MW00848768

IMPERILED (JAKE AND CHELSEA #2)

MELISSA F. MILLER

BROWN STREET BOOKS

Copyright © 2022 by Melissa F. Miller

All rights reserved.

No part of this book may be reproduced in any form or by any electronic or mechanical means, including information storage and retrieval systems, without written permission from the author, except for the use of brief quotations in a book review.

1

She was underground. She had to be. Chelsea had determined she was being held captive in a basement. The lack of windows was the first clue. The persistent background scent of soil and the damp cold that seeped through the paneled walls confirmed it. Along with the chill, the realization that her friend and employee had betrayed her was finally sinking in.

She'd known Vance Asher for years. She'd liked him. She'd trusted him. Relied on him.

She snorted at the absurdity of her situation. First, he'd gotten her business mixed up with a money-laundering ring. Then he'd managed to lose a client in the woods. And, finally, he'd assaulted and abducted her in a misguided effort to get her to give him a flash drive that she didn't even have.

Some judge of character you are.

She pressed her palm against the paneling. On the other side of this wall was the outdoors. Dirt and rock. Above that, grass, trees, water, sunlight. All things she desperately wanted to touch, smell, and see again.

Calm down. You've been in here, what, not even ten hours? You're going to get out of here.

She took a steadying breath. She would get out. She had to.

She checked her watch—just past eight o'clock in the morning. Vance had left over an hour ago, after tossing her an energy bar and a lukewarm bottle of water. She'd devoured the bar but had nursed the water. She hoped to avoid availing herself of the porcelain chamber pot as long as possible.

She trailed her hand along the cold paneling, then sank into the rocking chair in the corner of the small room. She rocked back and forth, back and forth, as she ran through her options for escaping the basement. None of them were great.

She could surprise Vance when he returned

—overpower him and scramble upstairs, then get the hell out of his house. But she didn't have a weapon. And, between choking her out and backhanding her hard enough to draw blood, he'd already shown he was perfectly willing to resort to physical violence. She wasn't sure how far he'd go, and she didn't want to find out.

She could bust through the paneling and try to dig her way out. But she didn't have any tools. And most homes in the region were constructed on fieldstone foundations. Even if she could find something to use to break through the paneling and access the stone wall, it'd take ages to tunnel out—like, a life sentence/*Shawshank Redemption* amount of time. Time she didn't have.

She could wait to be rescued. But there was an excellent chance nobody knew she was missing. Unless he was very, very stupid, Vance had moved her car from the parking lot and opened the store for business as usual. There was a real chance nobody would realize she was missing until next week, when she failed to keep her appointment for a dental cleaning.

No, her best—and, possibly, only—shot at getting out of here alive was to give Vance what he wanted. All she had to do was tell him where he could find the flash drive he wanted so badly. It was too bad she didn't have the faintest idea what he was talking about.

∼

J ake strolled through the parking lot, a travel mug of breakfast blend in one hand and his mind on his upcoming day. Then he heard the footsteps behind him. He kept walking but listened hard. The footsteps sped up. His pursuer kept up a determined clip. Headed straight for him.

He tensed and turned, acutely aware of the handgun strapped to his ankle. Old habits died hard. Even in the middle of nowhere, even on his own campus—in a location that appeared on no maps.

As he rotated, he caught a glimpse of bouncy, blonde hair and his brain registered the height and weight of his pursuer. He exhaled and raised his coffee mug in the universal gesture of commuters the world over to greet one of his newest hires—Olivia Santos.

"Morning, Olivia." He scanned the lot behind her. "Where's Trent?"

She closed the distance between them with several quick strides and raised her own mug to return his greeting. "We drove in separately. He's probably already inside."

He squinted and studied her face. Her blue eyes were clear and her forehead was smooth, but there was a slight, almost imperceptible, tightness around her eyes. He recognized the signs from his time serving as her security consultant. Olivia might hide it well, but she was *this* close to jumping out of her skin.

"What's wrong?"

She blinked, started to shake her head as if she might deny that she was upset, but then laughed. "Nothing gets by you, huh? I stopped by the outfitters to check on Chelsea."

She fell into step beside him.

His pulse thumped in the side of his throat at the mention of Chelsea. "Is she okay?"

Chelsea Bishop was one of the toughest women he'd ever met—and that included all the female military officers and law enforcement agents he'd worked with over the years. She didn't *look* especially formidable. In fact, she looked the exact opposite. With her long hair hanging down her back in plaits, her smattering of freckles, and her makeup-free face, she looked like what she was on the surface: a fresh-faced outdoor guide in a tiny town.

That easygoing, all-natural exterior hid a core of pure steel. Even so, she *was* a civilian. And she'd been through one hell of an ordeal. They'd been ambushed in the Shenandoah wilderness by desperate, armed men. She'd stabbed one of them and probably saved Jake's life in the process. Not to mention having to rescue her guide, Vance, and the fact that her client was still missing. In light of all that had happened, Jake wouldn't be surprised to hear Olivia say the emotional and physical toll of the past two days had caught up with her cousin.

What if that's not the emotional toll that's hit her? What if your insistence on dredging up the past has pushed her away? What if she's moved on?

He dismissed the thought and absently reached into his pocket, where the ring he intended to give Chelsea when the time was right sat, waiting.

No. She'd felt it, too. All the water under the bridge hadn't washed away the connection between them. She'd said as much. She just wanted to take it slowly, and he'd honor that. He had to.

Olivia snapped her fingers close to his face. "Hello? Did you hear me?"

He blinked and cleared his throat. "Sorry. One more time?"

She arched an eyebrow and studied him for an uncomfortably long moment before repeating herself. "I said, I don't *know* if she's okay. She wasn't at her shop."

"Oh."

"Oh?" Her voice vibrated with suppressed emotion. What was he missing?

"Yeah, oh. Maybe she slept in. You know, we didn't exactly get a good night's sleep in that cave."

He hadn't, at least. How could he? Not while sharing a sleeping bag with Chelsea. Not with her warm body curved into his. Not with her lavender-scented hair tickling his neck. He shook his head to dislodge the memory and forced himself to focus on Oliva, who was frowning at him.

"She didn't sleep in. She's not at her place. She's not answering her phone."

His stomach twisted. "That's ... odd."

"It is. And Vance was completely unhelpful. He said—"

He paused to pass his security fob in front of the door reader and turned toward her. "You saw Vance? Where?"

"At the outfitters. Why?"

The door clicked open. Olivia waved her fob at the reader so her arrival would also be recorded, and he ushered her inside the building ahead of him.

"He's supposed to be at the hospital. I thought they wanted to observe him for at least twenty-four hours."

"Well, he was at work, and he claimed to have no idea where Chelsea was," she informed him as they headed down the deserted hallway.

He searched her face. "How concerned about this are you?"

She stared back at him, no longer bothering to hide the tension in her face. "How concerned are *you*? I know I'm not the only one who cares about Chelsea. My sixth sense is tingling. I don't know why, but I know something's wrong."

Jake checked his gut. He didn't like the idea of not knowing where Chelsea was, of not knowing if she was safe. At the same time, he had to respect her wishes. Just last night, she told him she'd call him when she was ready to take the next step. And he told her he'd wait. So he couldn't very well bust down her door or put a trace on her car or phone or do whatever it was Olivia was expecting him to do. Even if he desperately wanted to do exactly that.

He stopped in front of his office door and placed his free hand on her shoulder.

"I'm not concerned," he lied. He locked eyes with her and lowered his chin. "Your cousin's fine."

2

Chelsea was spiraling, on the verge of panicking. She stopped pacing the dank, damp room, closed her eyes, and just breathed. In. Out. In. Out. In. Out.

She didn't know how long she stood there, frozen in the middle of her prison, breathing. It could have been minutes or an hour. All she knew was she had to contain her racing thoughts, tamp down her mounting fear, and slow her wildly palpitating heart.

Calm, cool, and collected was the only way to survive a disaster. Rationally, she knew she had to maintain control of her emotions. And she'd done it countless times. On the side of a mountain, on a trail, in a cave, deep in the woods. She'd faced down bears, avalanches, and wildfires.

But this was a different threat. She was trapped in a manmade cell, being held captive by a man who was both desperate and unpredictable—a dangerous, possibly even deadly, combination.

This isn't helping, she told herself as her pulse rate doubled. *Focus on something that will settle your nerves.*

Jake West popped into her mind, and she opened her eyes. Jake was an interesting choice, considering he set her pulse thrumming and her heart thumping. She pushed aside her physical attraction to consider how Jake would react if he found himself in this situation. He'd stay calm. That much she knew. And he'd stay positive. He'd radiate a conviction that he could get out of this basement. And if Jake could do it, she could too.

Right, sure. Because just like Jake, you're an Air Force Pararescue Specialist. How could you forget that you, too, underwent years of specialized training devoted to getting out of messes like this one?

She shook her head. Sarcasm wasn't going to help. She had to believe, sincerely believe, she could escape. Because she *could*. Maybe not the way Jake would, by busting through the limestone foundation or something. But she could think her way out of this trap. She just needed to relax so the tsunami of cortisol pounding through her veins would abate and she could actually think.

She held the image of Jake in her mind like a North Star or a touchstone to guide her. She needed to escape because she'd just found Jake again. After the long years of denying the effect he had on her and her heart, she'd finally admitted to herself that she still loved him. Now they had a second chance, and she'd be damned if she was going to miss out on it by dying in Vance Asher's depressing basement.

"Okay, think," she said aloud. Her voice echoed off the walls and bounced back, distorted and tense.

Vance was presumably in trouble with Royce Reynolds' partners because they wanted whatever was on the missing flash drive. All she had to do was convince Vance that she could help him out of his jam, and then, maybe, she'd be able to get out of hers.

Come on, think. Where would the flash drive

be? If Vance didn't have it, and the men who'd come after her and Jake in the woods didn't have it, then Royce must've taken it with him when he ran. Or he'd hidden it somewhere in the vast Shenandoah Wilderness. But where?

She rolled through her memories of the day and night in the woods. Royce's gear had vanished along with the man. Vance had dragged his pack up to the cave with him before collapsing from the blow to his head. If the drive had been in Vance's bag, she wouldn't be here. So Royce had either taken the drive with him or stashed it somewhere in the woods.

Great. No problem. The Shenandoah Wilderness only encompasses about eighty-thousand acres of land. Should be a piece of cake to find.

She barked out a bitter laugh that tiptoed right up to the edge of hysterics. Then a thought sparked in her mind and she smiled a genuine smile.

She didn't need to find the flash drive. She just needed to convince Vance that she *could.*

∾

Jake tossed the background material on a potential new security client onto his desk, leaned back, and cracked his neck —first one side, then the other. He'd read the same paragraph four times and had absorbed exactly nothing about the proposed assignment. His eyes scanned the words, but his thoughts were preoccupied. His mind was on Chelsea, shifting back and forth in a constant push-and-pull between worry and dismissal.

He wasn't going to accomplish a single blasted thing at this rate. He eyed the mug weighing down the stack of papers on the corner of his desk. There was a quarter-cup of coffee in it. He grabbed the mug and took a swig, then grimaced. Room temperature.

In the stairwell en route to the office kitchen, he ran into Potomac's general counsel. Almost literally. Ryan was walking down the stairs and reading at the same time, head bent over some papers, and nearly collided with Jake. Jake pivoted out of Ryan's path, then caught him by the elbow.

"Hey."

Ryan startled and raised his head. His eyes

grew wide behind his glasses. "Oh, sorry. Didn't see you."

"Yeah, I figured. It's only a matter of time before you do a header down a flight of stairs with your head buried in ... whatever you're reading."

Ryan grinned. "My mother's been saying that for almost three decades, man. Although back then, it was fantasy novels, not legal documents. But I'm still standing. I guess I've developed echolocation."

Jake forced a laugh.

Ryan cocked his head and studied him. "You okay?"

"Sure."

Ryan twitched his lips, unconvinced.

Jake suppressed a frown. He wasn't okay, but ought to be better at hiding it. It was one thing for one of his analysts or operatives to read his mood. But Ryan was a far cry from an analyst. Or an operative. No, his lawyer was the company's resident absent-minded professor. If Ryan noticed something was amiss, Jake had to be telegraphing it for the world to see.

"Actually," he amended, "I'm worried about Chelsea."

"Oh, that's funny. I'm on my way to your office. I have an update in her case."

"You do? She's been located?"

Ryan drew his eyebrows together. "Located? I didn't know she was missing."

"She's not. Or ... maybe she is. I don't know. What do you have?"

"The detective assigned to her case sent over Vance Asher's witness statement and a statement from the financial services company up in Boston where Reynolds works. Or worked, at least."

"Worked, past tense? They've already decided he's dead?"

"More like they've already decided he's dead to them. They've terminated him."

"That's cold. The man's missing."

Ryan gave him a look. "So is four-point-two million dollars."

Jake let out a long, low whistle. "He stole four million and change?"

"Well, he stole holdings worth four million and change," Ryan clarified.

"And this isn't the money he was laundering for the bad guys?"

"Nope, this is on top of that."

A thick silence settled over the stairwell.

After a moment, Jake said, "Reynolds has a compelling reason to disappear."

"I'd say he has about four million compelling reasons."

"So we think he's alive and hiding." That was good—for Chelsea. It meant her client hadn't died.

"Right. Marielle's team has already set up trackers on all his known bank accounts and credit cards, but ..."

"But he has the know-how and the resources to evade those traces."

Ryan nodded. "Sorry the news isn't better."

"At least we know what we're dealing with now."

"True. You want copies of these reports?"

"Yeah, when you get a chance."

Ryan slid a manila folder out from the bottom of his stack of papers and handed it to Jake. "One step ahead of you, boss."

"Thanks."

He tucked the folder under his arm. Too bad Royce Reynolds was also a step ahead of him.

3

The roar of Vance's Jeep as it rattled over the unpaved driveway jarred Chelsea out of her daydream. She wished she could say she was fantasizing about her escape, but the truth was, she was fantasizing about a burger. And fries.

It was funny how, when she was busy at the shop, she sometimes worked straight through lunch and dinner without realizing it. But stick her in an empty room with nothing to do, and all she could think about was her next meal.

The door upstairs creaked open, then slammed shut. She raised her eyes to the ceiling beams and followed Vance's footsteps as he walked overhead. The footsteps paused. A cabinet banged open and then shut. Was he in the pantry? He must've closed the shop and come home for lunch. Would he feed her, too?

If so, please, please, let him give me something more substantial than another energy bar.

Forget about food. Focus on Vance. She took a centering breath and leveled her gaze at the metal door. Her captor pounded down the stairs, his boots heavy on the wooden steps. As the deadbolt dragged across the door with a long *snick*, she arranged her face into an approximation of a smile.

Vance burst into the room fast, like he expected her to be waiting to lunge at him, and slammed the door shut behind him. She sat unmoving against the wall, watching.

"Hi."

He eyed her. "What are you so happy about?"

She wasn't happy. Not even close. But she *had* just gained valuable information.

The door doesn't lock from the inside. Only from the outside.

Which meant Vance's moment of maximum exposure would come when he unlocked the door and stepped inside. Although he'd be most vulnerable then, he'd also be on high alert and difficult to surprise.

But the door doesn't lock from the inside.

She had to bide her time, lull him into a false sense of security, and then ...

"Hello? Earth to Chelsea."

He was staring at her, and she realized she was staring at the door behind him. She blinked and shifted her gaze.

"Sorry. You know, I get spacey when I'm hungry. Is that a package of peanut butter crackers?" She nodded toward his hands.

He studied her for another moment before tossing the plastic-covered rectangle in her direction. "Yeah. Crackers and a bottle of water."

She caught the crackers and placed them in her lap, then reached out for the water. He crossed the small cell and extended his arm to give her the bottle, careful to maintain his distance.

She twisted off the cap and took a long swig of the cold water.

"Thanks. And I don't mean to be ungrateful, but I'm pretty hungry. I don't think a pack of snack crackers is really gonna get the job done."

She kept her tone matter-of-fact and free of complaint.

As if to drive the point home, her stomach chose that moment to rumble—a loud, long growl.

He frowned.

She smiled again. "You haven't really thought through how this is going to work, have you?"

Her understanding tone must've caught him off-guard. "No, I haven't," he admitted.

She let out a long breath. "Look, you reacted last night. I get it, I surprised you. And you're obviously in a bad spot. Let me help you."

He almost nodded, then jerked his head to a stop. "All I need from you is the damned drive."

"Vance, you have to listen to me. I don't know what you're talking about."

He shook his head. "I don't believe you."

She spread her hands wide. "Just think for a minute. How do *you* know there's a drive?"

"Those guys who came after Reynolds. They brought us all into the hospital at around the same time. The one you stabbed, he was in pretty bad shape. Everyone was rushing around trying to stabilize him, and the police officer was distracted. He was talking to a nurse about securing a wing, and the other guy grabbed my sleeve." Vance paused and lowered his gaze so that his eyes bored into hers. "He hissed in my ear. He said, 'Reynolds is a dead man because he stole from the wrong people. And if you don't return it, you're a dead man, too.'"

She shivered involuntarily. "And this thing they want is a flash drive? I thought Royce stole a lot of money."

"I'm just telling you what he told me. He said Royce Reynolds stole from the wrong people and then he said to return 'it.' But I didn't have any idea what 'it' was, so I asked him. And then the cop saw him talking to me and pulled him away. While he was being dragged away, he shouted that he was going to get the flash drive one way or another. So I *assume* the flash drive is what Royce stole, but I guess he could've been talking about the money." He shrugged. "Who cares about the details? Bad men want a drive that Reynolds had when we went into the woods. And they're not going to stop until they get it."

She studied his face, taking in his trembling lip and his tight eyes. "Those guys, the ones from the woods, they're in police custody. So who has you so spooked?"

He swallowed. When he spoke, his voice was soft, barely above a whisper.

"After dinner, I was sleeping. They'd put me in a private room for observation. The Boston guy was on another floor. The nurses had just done a shift change. It was quiet, deserted. This guy comes into my room, says he's gotta draw blood for labs. He's wearing scrubs, has an ID dangling from his neck on a lanyard, the whole deal." He paused and gulped, then continued, "He puts one of those elastic bands around my arm, ties it really tight, and pulls out a needle. I didn't think anything of it until he leaned over and whispered that his syringe was loaded with a drug that would stop my heart instantly."

Chelsea gasped.

Vance gave her a grim look. "For a second or two, I thought he was just a phlebotomist with a dark sense of humor. Then I realized he wasn't kidding. He told me I had until the end of the week to return the drive, untied the band, and walked out of the room. Once I stopped shaking, I took off. Checked myself out against medical advice."

He fell silent.

Chelsea's throat tightened as her reality sunk

in: Vance wasn't just desperate. He was trapped. And she wasn't going to be able to reason her way out of this. At this moment, he was no different from a cornered animal. He'd do whatever it took to ensure his survival, up to and including sacrificing her life to save his.

She managed a shaky breath. "I can't imagine how scary that was. But we're friends, Vance. If you'd told me what was going on, you know I'd help you any way I could."

He winced, and a shadow of guilt clouded his face. "I was freaked out. After I bolted from the hospital, I went straight to the outfitters. When you burst in, I thought ..."

"You thought I was him."

He nodded, and his face softened. For a moment, it seemed he might apologize, then he narrowed his eyes and snapped, "Yes. Why don't give it to me so we can end this already?"

"I don't have it, Vance. Don't you think I'd give it to you if I did? I'm telling you the truth—I don't have their drive. I don't understand why they're so sure Royce left it behind, anyway. Wouldn't he take it with him if it's so important?"

When he answered, his tone was a mixture of pity and disbelief. "Are you serious? I assume they have Royce. And if they have him, and they don't have the stupid drive, then he must've left it behind."

Her heart ticked up a beat as she realized he was right and, more critically, that the situation offered her a way out. "Well, if he doesn't have it, and you and I don't have it ... then it must still be in the woods. You know the wilderness areas better than anyone—except for me. I can help you find it. Take me to the woods and we'll find it together."

He twisted his mouth to the side and studied her, considering the idea. She kept her face blank and silently pleaded, '*Please, please, please.*'

She was out of her element in Vance's dank basement. But if she could get him to take her out to the woods, they'd be on equal footing, and she'd stand a fighting chance.

Please, please, please.

The seconds dragged on. Vance eyed her. She fought to keep her face an impassive mask. Finally, right when she thought she might scream, he shrugged.

"It's not like I have a better idea. Let's go."

4

Jake found Olivia and Trent in the canteen, holding court at a table full of junior employees. He suppressed an eye roll. The few people at Potomac Private Services who hadn't already hero-worshipped Trent had joined the masses when Olivia entered the picture. There was nothing as effective at burnishing a man's reputation as the love of a gorgeous, accomplished woman. Reflected glory.

A wry chuckle died in Jake's throat. He could snark on Trent all day long, and sometimes he did just that. After all, someone had to keep Trent's ego in check, and who better for the job than his best friend?

To his credit, Trent took the ribbing in stride.

He knew Jake was happy for him. Because Jake, more than anyone, knew the demons Trent had fought to find Olivia—and happiness.

And Jake *was* happy for him. Of course he was. But, the full truth—the ugly truth that whispered to Jake in the pre-dawn hours—was that he was also jealous of Trent. He yearned for what Trent and Olivia had. He wanted it for himself. He wanted it with Chelsea.

Automatically, he dipped his hand into his pocket, and his fingers closed around the simple silver band that he carried everywhere now.

She didn't say no, he reminded himself. *She said not yet.*

Her hedging had stung. But the heat in her green eyes when she told him she wanted to take things slowly was real, and it had soothed his pride. He and Chelsea belonged together. He knew it, and she knew it. She just needed to pick up the phone. Until then, Jake had to make his peace with the Chelsea-shaped hole in his life.

The sudden absence of noise arising from Trent and Olivia's table cut through his thoughts. He blinked and focused to see a row of faces looking at him with naked curiosity. He coughed into his elbow, then stepped forward and clasped Trent on the shoulder.

"Is this guy regaling you with stories about his heroic adventures?" Jake addressed the question to one of the new hires, but Trent answered it.

"Nah, man. I'm telling them what a badass Olivia is."

Olivia arched one perfectly groomed eyebrow and nodded. "It's true. I *am* pretty amazing."

She laughed, then squinted up at Jake. Her mouth creased into a frown, and she tapped Trent's wrist with two fingers.

Some unspoken understanding passed between them, and Trent made their excuses to their rapt audience, while Olivia pitched their compostable lunch trays into the barrel that Chelsea had hassled Jake into providing. She'd partnered up with some local environmental group to convince businesses in the Shenandoah Valley to join a composting and recycling program. It was darn near impossible to say no to her, and the Valley had an eighty-percent participation rate. He chuckled softly at the memory of how she'd stood in his doorway, persuading him.

Now her cousin hovered by a different doorway with Trent by her side. She cocked her head toward the hallway. Jake nodded a goodbye to the group at the table and joined them. She pulled him by the sleeve out into the corridor.

"What is it?" Her voice was level.

"I have an update on Royce Reynolds, and I think your cousin should know about it. Have you heard from her yet?"

Olivia's clear blue eyes clouded. "No. I told you this morning, it's like she's fallen off the face of the earth."

"Have you tried to reach her again?"

She twisted her lips. "No, Jake. I just threw my hands up and said, oh, well. Of course, I've tried to get ahold of her again. I've been calling her all morning at every number I have for her."

His gut tightened. "And nothing?"

She shook her head. "Crickets."

He fell silent, thinking.

Trent cleared his throat. "What's going on, bro? Liv said you blew her off this morning about Chelsea, and now you're on high alert."

Jake didn't bother denying it. Every alarm

bell in his brain clanged like a klaxon, his pulse thrummed, and adrenaline washed through his veins.

"Those guys that Reynolds was mixed up with are bad news."

"Yeah, money launderers. We know."

"More than that. Apparently, Reynolds stole several million dollars from their brokerage account before he vanished. If they think she knows where that money is ..." He trailed off, unable or unwilling to complete the thought.

"Chelsea could be in danger," Trent finished the sentence for him.

"About time," Olivia muttered under her breath.

Her fiancé shot her a warning look, then turned back toward Jake. "Why don't you and I drive over to Chelsea's place and just have a look around."

"I'm coming, too." Olivia fisted her hands on her hips and jutted her chin out, eyes blazing as she dared them to tell her no.

Trent eyed Jake. It was his call.

"Listen, I'm sorry I didn't take you more seriously this morning. That was my mistake. I let my feelings about your cousin cloud my judgment. But, I'm on board now. I'll find her and make sure she's okay—"

She opened her mouth to interrupt him, and he raised his hand to ward her off.

"—I need you to stay here and handle a meeting for me."

"Why? Take me, and let Trent cover the meeting. He's your second-in-command, isn't he?"

He was, and that was why Jake needed him to come along. If he ran into trouble, he wanted Trent to have his back. Trent would anticipate his moves, like a dance partner. The connection between members of a team was hard to put into words.

Olivia was more than competent. She *was* a badass. But she was new to his team, and they didn't have the copacetic, instinctive understanding that he and Trent had. She'd operated as a lone wolf for years with the CIA as a NOC. Operatives working under non-official cover don't have anyone to cover their backs. They're alone on a high-wire without a net. That experience had made her tough and fearless, but it hadn't made her a team player. And, for that reason, she was the very *last* person he'd take for backup.

He wasn't stupid enough to say any of this to Olivia Santos.

Instead, he nodded. "He is, but this client needs special treatment. Your experiences with your, uh, ex-husband make you uniquely qualified to take point on this."

"Why? Is the client a gaslighting, emotionally abusive adulterer?" Trent interjected.

Olivia swallowed a laugh.

"No, but he is a multimillionaire. Hell, he could be a billionaire for all I know. He's an oilman. Lots of dealings with the Saudis, the UAE. He's got a skyscraper named after him in Dubai. Olivia's the only person working here who's been married to a millionaire with extensive international dealings—at least as far as I know."

Olivia pursed her lips, pretending to consider this information. But Jake saw the flash of interest in her eyes, and Trent did, too. They all knew Jake was handing her a plum assignment and demonstrating her importance to Potomac.

She clicked her tongue against her teeth. "Okay, but I hate him already."

Jake laughed. "Fair enough. The file's on my desk. You can go in and grab it." He checked his watch. "He'll be here in about an hour."

"Gee, thanks for all the warning so I can prep." She turned to leave, then looked over her shoulder. "Please find my cousin."

"We will," Jake vowed, hoping it was a promise he could keep.

Trent drove, as usual. Jake clutched the grab bar, as usual. As Trent careened around the bend in Falls Road, Jake smothered a yelp.

"Are you channeling Leilah Khan? Slow down. This isn't the track."

Trent just grinned and nailed the throttle. Jake tightened his grip on the handle. As they passed Chelsea's outfitters up on the hill, a blur of black and white somehow registered in Jake's brain.

"Stop!"

"Dude, I'm a certified defensive driving instructor. You're safer in a car with me than you are sitting on your freaking couch. Anyway, when did you turn into such a—"

"Stop!" Jake roared.

Trent jammed down on the brakes, bringing the truck to a squealing stop in the middle of the road. Jake released his grip on the bar, threw his hands out in front, and braced himself against the dashboard.

"Happy?"

"Seriously? You're out of control. Anyway, there's a patrol car in the parking lot." He jerked his head toward Chelsea's store.

Trent glanced in the rearview mirror, then nodded. "I'm impressed you saw it. I mean, I took that curve going eighty, easy."

"I'm aware," Jake said dryly.

"You wanna go check it out?"

"Yeah. You better hope that new patrol officer isn't sitting up there with a radar gun, hunting for speeders."

Trent threw the gear into reverse and sped backward down the road. As he turned into the lot, he cracked, "I think we're safe. It's early in the month. They don't start shooting fish in a barrel until they're closer to their quota."

Jake nodded. He knew. Oh, did he know. For

a company made up mainly of former military and law enforcement folks, his people were remarkably lax about following the speed limit. Speeding tickets made up a significant line item in Potomac's budget. He groused about it, but the truth was, the local PD saw Potomac as a cash cow and treated Jake like a major donor.

Trent zipped through the parking lot and pulled up next to the squad car. He killed the engine.

"Pretty sure this isn't an actual parking spot," Jake observed.

Trent shrugged. "Close enough."

As they walked around to the front of the building, Jake noted that aside from Trent's pickup and the black and white sedan, there wasn't another car in the lot. He frowned. They turned the corner and nearly bumped into Bruce Halloran, the rookie police officer on the local force.

"Oh, sorry, guys!" Bruce lifted his head from his logbook just before he bumped into the granite wall that was Jake's chest.

"No worries, Officer Halloran." Jake smiled easily.

"Officer," Trent nodded in greeting.

"Uh, hi, Mr. West, Mr. Mann."

Officer Halloran was all of twenty, and no matter how many times Jake told him to dispense with the formalities, he persisted in calling Jake 'Mr. West.'

"Is something going on in there?" Jake gestured toward the entrance to the store.

"Oh, no. They're closed for lunch."

Trent slid Jake a sidelong look. Jake shrugged. Chelsea didn't close for lunch. But, then, if Vance was covering for her, he might need a break. He *had* just been through quite an ordeal.

"So, what are you doing here, then?"

Jake took advantage of Halloran's inexperience to press him for answers a more experienced officer would never give a civilian.

"Uh, Ms. Bishop called in a burglary last night. I wanted to get her statement."

Jake's chest tightened, and his blood roared in his ears. *What happened last night?*

He felt Trent's eyes on him as he tried to strike a casual tone. "Who responded to the call last night? Wouldn't they have taken a statement?"

Halloran dropped his gaze to his feet and

mumbled, "Nobody came out last night. We couldn't spare a unit, uh ... you know, with the storm and all the flooding. She called it in, and the emergency dispatcher told her someone would stop by sometime today." He looked up. "But she's not here."

Jake struggled to think. His mind raced. "What time was this?"

"What? I mean, what, sir?" Halloran tripped over the words.

"When did she call? She was with us at The Falls until at least ten-thirty, maybe a little before eleven. And she said she was going straight home from there. I walked her to her car." Jake volunteered the last bit of information more for Trent's benefit than for the police officer's.

Halloran flipped back to an earlier page in his log book. "Dispatch has the time of the call as eleven oh seven."

Trent grunted. "She probably came this way from the restaurant. She'd have been driving right by at that time."

"You think she spotted someone trying to get in when she crested the hill? At that time of night?"

"You spotted Officer Halloran's squad car

while we were coming around that bend at high speed," Trent countered. Then he assured the rookie officer, "Not *too* fast."

Jake tried to picture the scene. Chelsea, tired and tense, driving along the darkened road. She rounds the bend, glances up the hill toward her store out of habit, and something catches her eye. "She saw a light on inside."

"Or a car in the lot," Trent countered.

"Could be. But I doubt it. The lot would have been pitch black." He pointed behind them. "No exterior lights."

Halloran scanned his notes. "It says here she told the operator she could see someone inside, moving around." He swallowed and continued reading, "Dispatch informed the caller that no units were available to respond due to weather conditions. Caller was assured an officer would stop by the next day. Caller objected and was advised that human life was the department's priority. Dispatch ended call to keep line clear for true emergencies."

The officer kept his head bent and stared down at his notebook unblinkingly. Trent and Jake exchanged a knowing look.

"What'd you think? Would she go inside

herself after the cops blew her off?" Trent didn't bother sugarcoating the question.

Halloran blanched.

Jake's heart banged against his rib cage. He had to work up some saliva to spit out an answer. "I know she would. That store's her life. She's a business owner. You think if I saw someone breaking into our offices there's any chance I'd walk away?"

"No, but—"

"—But what? I'm a PJ, so it's different? No." Jake shook his head. "I *know* her. I know she went inside. She's tougher than she looks."

"Whoa, whoa, easy." Trent placed a hand on Jake's tense arm. "I'm not doubting you. I'm sure she's a complete badass. I mean, after all, she shares DNA with Olivia."

Jake exhaled. "Sorry. I'm worried."

"I know, man. I am, too."

The police officer studied them, his eyebrows knitting together. "Am I missing something?"

"Yeah, Halloran, you are. Chelsea Bishop's missing. The last time anyone heard from her was that 9-1-1 call," Jake bit off the words.

"Oh."

"Yeah, oh."

Officer Halloran ran a finger around the inside of his collar, then scratched his neck. "So, uh, what should we do?"

Jake closed his eyes and counted to three. Then he opened them and growled, "You go back to the station and let a grown-up know the burglary in progress they dismissed has blown up into a potential abduction."

Halloran gulped. "Yes, sir."

Trent interjected in an only slightly less aggressive tone, "We're going to run down a lead, and then we'll head into the station ourselves to brief the force. Make sure the supervising officer on duty is up to date on the situation when we get there. Understand?"

"Y-yes. Are you sure you don't want me to come with you? You know, for backup?"

Before Trent could respond, Jake laughed darkly. "No, Halloran, we don't need backup. You all have done enough, by which I mean, absolutely nothing."

He stalked back to the car without waiting for a response. He fisted his hands and clenched his jaw. A wave of shame for tearing into the rookie washed over him. He prided himself on not punching down. Leading and bullying weren't synonyms.

But much as he hated to admit it, he didn't seem to be able to control himself. Chelsea was missing. Four million dollars was missing. And Royce Reynolds was missing. Until he could get some answers, Jake knew his fear would manifest as anger, and his anger would build. He needed to find the woman he loved before he exploded on someone for real.

5

Chelsea stumbled over the path, clumsy and off-balance with her wrists duct-taped together. Vance walked behind her, prodding her forward when her pace slowed.

"Hey, Vance, is this necessary?" She turned and raised her bound arms. "I mean, really?"

He gave her a sour look. "Yes. We both know if you get your hands on a rock or a branch or something and give me a knock on the head, you could disappear into these woods and nobody would find you unless you wanted them to."

She tilted her head. "Is that what Royce Reynolds did?"

"What?"

"He hit you in the head with the oar and then took off, didn't he?"

"Yes. Maybe. I don't know. I told you, I was taking a leak, it was dark. Someone came up behind me and bashed my brains in." His hand hovered near his temples as if he were reliving the blow. "Could've been Royce. Could've been those goons from Boston. It doesn't matter, does it? When I came to, Royce was gone."

She studied him a moment longer, then nodded. "I guess it doesn't."

She pivoted to face the clearing and gestured with her useless hands. "That boulder up ahead, that's where I found the emergency beacon. It was sitting on the rock, almost like you left it there on purpose."

"I told you, I didn't leave it there."

"Okay, almost like *someone* left it there on purpose."

As soon as the words left her lips, Chelsea realized what they meant. She hurriedly turned back to the clearing, smoothed her expression into a neutral mask, and prayed Vance hadn't caught the significance.

He jabbed his finger into the small of her back. "We don't have all day. Move it. We need to look around that big rock. See if there's any trace of the drive."

She closed her eyes and exhaled a long, slow breath. *He didn't catch it. He doesn't know.*

She walked haltingly toward the boulder, pushing her excitement down, and pretended to scan the area for a flash drive. The still-damp silt gave way under her feet, spongy with undrained stormwater. Behind her, Vance's boots squelched loudly, and he swore under his breath.

She circled the rock and swept her eyes over the ground. "I don't see anything here. I guess that makes sense—he wouldn't have left it out in the open. Maybe in that thicket?" She cocked her head toward a dense patch of holly.

Vance eyed the brush. She knew what he was thinking. Holly bushes had evolved an amazing defense mechanism to stave off hungry animals. Although the holly sold in commercial nurseries each December was known for its distinctive red berry surrounded by smooth, shiny green leaves, in the wild, holly was a favorite snack for deer. And after a deer munched on a holly plant, the new leaves that grew would not be smooth.

Instead, the plant would modify itself and grow sharp, jagged leaves to surround and protect the new holly berry. The Shenandoah wilderness was loaded with deer and, consequently, loaded with barbed holly leaves that poked and stung like thorns when an animal or person brushed up against them.

"Ugh. Do you really think Royce would've hidden it in there?" He blanched at the thought of crawling through the berry brambles.

She raised an eyebrow. "It's the perfect spot. You don't want to go in there. Neither do I. Neither would anyone."

He bobbed his head from side to side, thinking. "That's a good point." His eyes flicked toward the holly patch and then back to Chelsea. He smiled.

"What?"

"You climb through that mess. I'll wait here."

She pretended to think about it. After a beat, she said, "I'll do it—if you free my hands."

He frowned.

She pressed the point. "Come on, Vance. I can't crawl around in that brush with my hands bound. Cut the tape off, and I'll do it."

He twitched his lips, then shrugged. "Sure, why not?"

She extended her hands, and he took his Swiss Army knife from his jacket pocket, flicked the serrated blade out, and sawed through the duct tape. As he worked, she glanced over at the holly patch and planned her moves, walking through each step in her mind.

He sliced through the tape and yanked it from her wrists with a flourish. "There."

She rubbed her hands over her raw, red skin. "Thanks."

He gave her a small push, and she stumbled toward the holly. "Go get 'em."

She pulled her sleeves down over her hands and pushed through two entwined plants. The leaves tore at her shirt and exposed skin, and she yelped and pulled back.

"Go on, then."

She grumbled and plunged deeper into the mess of thorny plants. She looked over her shoulder. She couldn't see Vance from where she stood. She dropped to the ground and scrabbled through the dirt and roots until she found a flattish, palm-sized rock. She hefted it, feeling the weight in her hand, then raised herself into a low crouch.

"Hey, Vance!" She called.

"Yeah?"

"I think I found something."

"So bring it to me."

"Uh, I can't. It's buried under this bush. I need your knife to dislodge it."

He laughed a cold laugh. It echoed through the silent woods. "Nice try. I'm not arming you. I'll get it out myself. Just give me a minute."

She took a long breath, steadied her hands, and tried to ignore the frenetic hammering of her heart. Vance crashed through the branches, yipping and swearing.

"Where are you?"

She kept her eyes on his form as he approached from her left. "I can see you. Walk straight toward my voice about twenty feet, then duck under a low-hanging branch. I'll be to your left."

"Left? You sure? It sounds like you're on my right." He stopped and cocked his head, listening.

"No, it's left. I'm sure," she lied. "The echoes distort things."

"I guess." After a moment, he resumed thrashing through the brush and muttering darkly.

As he drew closer, step by step, her resolve faltered. Could she really do this? Could she bash him in the head with a rock?

Yes, she told herself hotly. *You can, and you will.*

Four more steps, three more steps. He ducked under the low-hanging branch. Chelsea crouched just to his right, concealed by a dense bush that had thankfully been untouched by deer. Vance straightened to standing and brushed off his pants, then turned to his left, away from her hiding spot.

Now!

She sprang out from behind the bush and raised the rock. Vance turned at the noise as she swung her arm in an arc and smashed the rock down directly on the bandage covering the stitches from his last blow to the head.

His eyes rolled wildly from side to side as he let out a wordless roar. For a moment, his gaze seemed to focus on her.

"Wha—?"

She brought the rock up and bashed him

again. Blood oozed out from under his bandage and he staggered backward, pawing at his head. She lunged forward and shoved him with all her strength. He threw out his arms as he fell but failed to regain his balance. He landed in the middle of the thorny bush.

She didn't wait to see if he'd get up. She turned and ran. She ran without stopping until she reached the trailhead. Then she leaned against a tree to catch her breath and still her shaking legs. She looked over her shoulder every other breath, terrified that she'd see Vance lumbering toward her, but the trail was deserted. She saw no signs of life, not even a bird or squirrel. Finally, when she was sure he wasn't coming, she slid her back along the tree until she reached the cold, damp ground, pulled her knees in close to her chest, lowered her head, and cried.

She cried until her tears ran dry. Then she cried some more, taking great heaving breaths. When the horror of the last hours had passed, she filled her lungs with the crisp fall air and pulled herself to her feet.

Now what?

She hadn't had the presence of mind to reach into Vance's pocket and take his car keys.

That's not strictly true, she told herself. She'd thought of it, but she couldn't bring herself to do it. She was afraid that if she got that close to him, he'd convince her not to leave him.

She'd left him. She'd attacked Vance, then left him bleeding, injured, and possibly unconscious out in the elements.

Oh, God, what have I done? She pressed a hand to her mouth.

Then she heard Jake's voice in her mind. *You did what you had to do to save yourself. Good girl. Now get the hell out of there.*

She drew a deep breath, set her jaw, and started hiking toward the road that led to town. As she crested a small hill, she burst out laughing. Not forty-eight hours earlier, she'd risked her life to get an injured Vance out of these same woods. Now, she'd brought him back and left him. She should have saved herself the effort. She stopped and doubled over, hands on her thighs, and howled, her laughter veering toward hysterics.

Pull it together. The drive that Vance is so desperate to get his hands on is in the communicator.

It has to be. So you have to get it before he does. Walk into town and get a ride to the police station. Then you can have your nervous breakdown.

She straightened and resumed walking. One foot in front of the other. It was all she could do.

6

Jake clenched his teeth and stared out the windshield at the road ahead, the tightness in his jaw giving him a mild headache.

"What?" he said without turning to look at Trent.

"What?"

"I can feel you positively bursting to say something. Say it, before you explode."

In his peripheral vision, he saw Trent take his eyes off the road to glance at him. He continued to look straight ahead. After a moment, Trent turned his gaze back to the road.

"It's not his fault."

Jake waited, but Trent said nothing more.

"Who? Halloran?"

"Yeah."

"I know."

Trent glanced over again and cleared his throat. "You always say true leaders aren't bullies."

"I know what I say, Mann." He bit the words off.

"So you don't mean it?" Having broached the subject, Trent was apparently unwilling to drop it.

Jake stopped himself from squirming and turned to face his second-in-command and best friend. "No. I do mean it."

"So?"

He exhaled heavily. "So my emotions got the better of me."

"I wasn't aware you had emotions."

"Har har."

Trent punched him lightly on the shoulder. "Sorry, couldn't resist. So, Chelsea's not just an old flame?" His tone was deliberately casual.

Jake hesitated.

"Come on, man. It's blatant."

"What is?"

"You've got it bad for her. And if you're trying

to hide it, you need to brush up on your concealment skills. Maybe our resident covert agent can give you a refresher. Half the time, I have no idea what Olivia's thinking."

Jake threw back his head and laughed. "Yeah, I'll bet she's a hard nut to crack."

Trent laughed with him, then grew serious. "I mean it, though. What did you tell me about Carla?"

Jake blinked. Trent never brought up the topic of Carla Ricci, his partner on a two-member SEAL team and his lover. Carla'd been murdered to cover up a political scandal and Trent had nearly destroyed himself with regret and self-recrimination. He searched his memory for the last time he and Trent had talked about Carla.

It had been when Trent was playing a fool, shutting Olivia out. He'd told Trent that Carla wouldn't want him to live out his life as a miserable hermit.

"I told you Carla would want you to be happy," he said softly.

"Right," Trent said thickly.

He waited a beat. "I'm sorry, I don't know what you're driving at."

Trent threw him a disbelieving look. "You can't be that dense. You made me see that I couldn't let Carla's ghost stop me from admitting how I felt about Olivia. I took your advice, crawled out of the pit I'd buried myself in, and now look at me. I'm freaking engaged, man."

Jake cracked a smile. "Miracles do happen."

"And you're no different than I was. You might have everyone else fooled with your successful, beloved CEO routine—"

"—You forgot handsome."

"—Passable looking. But I'm not fooled, West. You're still in love with a girl you walked away from more than a decade ago. You're in denial."

He swallowed, then braced himself and said, "First of all, Chelsea's not a ghost. She's very much alive."

Trent shook his head. "Doesn't mean you aren't haunted."

Jake shrugged. It wasn't untrue. "But, second, I didn't walk away from Chelsea. She went out and didn't come back."

Trent opened his mouth to argue, but Jake raised his hand to forestall the interruption. "Let me finish. Third, I'm not in denial. The minute I laid eyes on her at the cabin where she stashed you and Olivia, I knew. You're right. I am still in love with her. Guess I always have been."

He kept his eyes on Trent's face as the words landed.

"Knew it!" He pumped his fist in triumph then slapped the steering wheel. "Olivia owes me twenty bucks."

"You two bet on this?"

"Yeah, but I bet on you! She kept insisting Chelsea's the one carrying a torch and ..."

"And what?"

"Uh, and that you're dead inside. But, she meant it in the nicest possible way."

Jake snorted. "Right."

After a short pause, Trent blurted, "So, you have to tell her, man. You can't keep something like that buried."

He coughed. "I did tell her. I told her last night."

Trent's eyes went wide. "And?"

"And she wants to take things slow, said she needs some time."

"Oh."

"Yeah. Oh. Anyway, I'm not in denial and I'm not dead inside."

No, he was exposed and vulnerable, like a newborn deer whose mother left it to go forage for food. One good blow, and he'd crumple to the ground on his unsteady legs, defenseless.

Trent fell silent, and Jake leaned his head back and closed his eyes. They rode in silence for several moments until they reached the fork in the road.

Trent hit the brakes. "You never said where we're going. Left to Chelsea's, I assume?"

He almost said yes, but his gut said no.

He opened his eyes. "No. Hang a right here and turn onto Old Mill Road."

Trent raised an eyebrow, but made the right turn. "What's on Old Mill Road?"

"Vance Asher's place."

"Huh. What's your thinking?"

Jake shook his head. "I'm not sure. But Asher told Olivia that Chelsea asked him to cover for her today. That makes him the last person to talk to her as far as we know. So, he's worth chatting with."

"Yeah, he is. And you think he went home for lunch, not into town?"

"It's a hunch, okay?"

"You're the boss."

"I didn't mean it that way. I just can't explain it, but I think we should go to his place."

Trent gave him a sidelong look. "I didn't take it any way. You *are* the boss. And your spidey senses are the stuff of legend. So let's do it."

Old Mill Road was a bumpy, unmaintained, sorry excuse for a road. It had never been a major thoroughfare, as far as Jake knew. Used mainly by the Valley and Mountain Lumber Mill, when the mill shut down, the road had been abandoned. As they rattled and bounced down the hill, he understood the allure of the new Mill Road—smooth and flat and unlikely to rattle a person's teeth in their mouth.

"Good gravy," Trent muttered.

"Guess we know why Vance drives a Jeep."

"No kidding. How much further is it?"

Jake closed his eyes to visualize the file Ryan had handed him. He pictured Vance Asher's statement and zoomed in on the address. He opened his eyes. "He's at 1204."

They each turned to scan the sides of the deteriorating road for mailboxes, which were few and far between. Finally, Trent spotted a rusted metal mailbox that had tilted so far to the side it seemed to be defying gravity. He turned his head sideways to read the numbers.

"1201. I think."

Jake leaned forward and peered through the windshield. "Then Vance's house should be just up here on the right."

"Should be," Trent agreed.

He slowed the car to a crawl, and Jake stared hard at the shoulder of the road.

"There's 1202."

They inched forward and around a curve in the road. The thin, scrubby trees that had lined the sides of the road until that point were suddenly replaced by dense, tall, old-growth trees, crowded together on both sides. Jake imagined that in the spring and summer, the branches would leaf out and hang over the road, creating a lush canopy. This time of year, though, the trees were mostly bare. Row after row of straight brown sticks reaching toward the sky, naked save for the stray dead leaf clinging desperately to a branch, refusing to give in to the inevitable change of the seasons. He knew how those stubborn leaves felt.

He shook his head. *What is wrong with you?*

Wax philosophical or have your existential crisis or whatever this is later. After you find Chelsea.

Suddenly his inner voice, which usually sounded suspiciously like his first drill sergeant, Frank King, shifted. Clear as bell, he heard Chelsea saying with a gentle tone, *You're not a dead leaf. But you are kind of an idiot. Focus.*

Trent eyed him, and Jake wondered if he'd said any of that aloud. He sincerely hoped not.

"There's no 1204, Jake. Look." Trent gestured ahead of them.

He was right. Row after row of hardwood trees stretched out before them for as far as the eye could see.

"We must've missed it. Turn around."

"We didn't miss it."

"Turn around," he repeated. It wasn't a request.

Trent shook his head, but palmed the wheel and guided the car onto a rutted path that peeked out from between the trees. He put it in reverse and was about to execute a flawless three-point turn when Jake saw it.

He grabbed Trent's forearm. "Wait."

Trent stopped.

Jake peered through the windshield, then

hopped out of the car and jogged a few yards down the steep overgrown path. Trent came up behind him.

Jake pointed at a small, dark shadow in the valley below. "Is that a house?"

Trent squinted. "Might be. Might not. There's only one way to find out."

They huffed back to the car.

Trent selected four-wheel drive and grinned. "Off-roading, yeah, boy!"

Jake clutched the grab bar and hung on as if his life depended on it. Which, to be fair, it probably did.

Trent whooped and hollered and careened over the rocks and hard-packed earth at high speed, and Jake thought of more peaceful times —like the time he jumped out of a helicopter into the Arctic Ocean or when he'd disarmed an IED on a dusty roadside while a cluster of little kids who refused to obey his orders to disperse chattered over his shoulder excitedly. Things like that.

Lost in his memories, he wasn't prepared when Trent stomped down on the brakes. A small, brown furry shape darted across the path. He lost his grip on the handle and pitched forward. His forehead thudded against the hard plastic dashboard and bounced off, throwing him back like a rag doll. Trent thrust out his arm and caught him before he hit the headrest and ricocheted back.

"Sorry, dude."

"Yeah." Jake shook his head to try to clear his blurred vision. That was a mistake. It hurt like the devil and did nothing to help him focus.

"You okay?"

"I'll be fine in a minute. Let's go."

Trent gave him a doubtful look.

"I'm fine."

"If you say so. You're the one with the medical training, not me."

"And you're the one with the driving training ... and yet, here we are."

It was a weak attempt at humor, but, to Jake's relief, Trent chuckled. That was good. He had to put on a good show and prevent Trent from realizing that he was very much *not* okay. At least until they found Chelsea.

"Sorry, a rabbit or something ran in front of us."

"A rabbit?"

"Could've been a groundhog."

Jake tried to laugh. "Not a deer?"

"Definitely not a deer."

"What's Leilah say? Oh, yeah, when you're driving at speed, small, furry things die."

Trent managed a sickly smile. "Sorry, dude. I just ... I didn't want to kill it."

Jake took a long, deep breath to quell his rising nausea. He swallowed, pushed the car door open, and gingerly walked to join Trent in the front of the car.

"You really think that's where Asher lives?" Trent pointed down the hill.

Jake looked in the general direction but he was still seeing double. "Could be. You have binoculars in the truck?"

"Sure. But, we don't need them. It's only—"

"Just grab them. Four million dollars is a lot of money. We're unlikely to be the only ones interested in Asher's whereabouts. Before we go down there and knock on his door, let's make sure we're not walking into an ambush."

"Good point."

It *was* a good point. It would have been better had he thought to make it before Trent *yee-hawed* his way down the road.

Trent jogged to the truck and returned a

moment later with a pair of high-powered field glasses.

He tried to hand the binoculars to Jake, but Jake waved him off. "Just tell me what you see."

He blinked, as if that might reset his vision, and tried to ignore the screaming, red-hot pain in his head while Trent dialed the magnification in to his liking.

"Okay. Looks like that house—well, it's more of a shack—is inhabited. There's a county trash bin on the side—you know, one of the new ones they made everybody buy last year."

"Good. Anything else?"

"There are no snipers up on the hill behind the house if that's what you're asking. But ... hang on ..." Trent trailed off.

Jake waited a beat. Trent was breathing too loud and too fast.

"What is it?"

"Uh ... here, take a look."

Trent thrust the binoculars into his hands. He jammed them up to his face and concentrated on clearing his vision. He could make out the house with its brown shingles. The green trash bin Trent had mentioned was little more than a blob.

"What am I looking for?"

"Behind the house, there's a depression and then the hill. There's a woodshed to the right of the house."

"Yeah?" He'd take Trent's word for it.

"Beside the shed, do you see that blue tarp?"

He shifted his gaze to the right and increased the magnification. "I see it."

"I think that's Chelsea's Forester peeking out from under the tarp."

Jake's throat constricted and his hands began to shake as a shot of pure adrenaline pumped through his veins. He swallowed hard and dialed up the magnification further. That was definitely Chelsea's perpetually muddy crossover vehicle.

Another wave of nausea rose up, and there was no holding this one back. He turned and emptied his stomach into the grass. He rested his hands on his thighs and dry heaved. The binoculars hung around his neck, banging against his chest with every heave. He wiped his mouth with the back of his hand and returned to standing.

"That is her car," he confirmed as if he hadn't just puked his guts out.

"So we have two problems."

"Two?"

"Yeah, Chelsea may be in trouble, and you have a concussion."

"I don't have—"

"Bull."

Jake sighed. Trent may not be an EMT, but everyone on Jake's team had basic medical training. Lying was pointless.

"Bravo, you caught me. I'll be fine in a few minutes. We have to get down there."

"No."

"It wasn't a request."

Trent gripped his shoulder. "I understand you want to spring into action. I get it, bro. But you need medical attention and—"

"—No."

Trent went on as if Jake hadn't spoken. "—and I'm not walking into a potentially dangerous situation with you, in this condition, as my backup."

Trent's words drove home the truth: Jake might be willing to rush into the breech, but he couldn't risk Trent's life. Because Trent was right —Jake wouldn't want himself as backup right now.

"Fine," he said heavily. "I'll get checked out. But we go to the police station first."

"But—"

"Not up for discussion." He handed the binoculars back to Trent and trudged to the truck.

7

Chelsea trudged along the berm of the highway. Her energy was flagging, and her mouth was bone dry. She was cold, tired, hungry, and dehydrated. She let out a shivery breath and estimated her distance to town. At least six miles to go. She pushed her rubbery legs to keep moving. One step at a time, each one harder than the last.

At this point, she was praying for a car to come by. If she could hitch a ride even part of the way, it would be a blessing. But the truth was, this road was lightly traveled under usual circumstances, and with the flooding and downed branches from the storm, many of the connecting roads were likely to be impassable. In other words, it would be a miracle if a car came by.

"Just keep walking. One foot after the other. You've got this." She spoke the words aloud in a firm, reassuring voice, as a memory from a lifetime ago came back to her.

It was the second or third week of their hike. She and Jake were halfway between two towns on the Pacific Coastal Trail. Their pack of food, hanging in a tree, had nonetheless been ransacked by raccoons during the night. After a fruitless argument over whether raccoons could climb trees, she and Jake had had to face their reality. They were out of food and twenty-some miles from the nearest place where they could re-provision.

So, there'd been nothing to do but keep walking. As they marched forward, they kept telling each other, 'Just keep walking. One foot after the other. We've got this.' Over and over, like a mantra. And it worked—for a few hours.

It had been an unusually warm day, almost hot. After a while Jake took off his shirt. She put aside her jealousy that he had that option long enough to admire his toned, tanned chest and abs and the defined muscles in his back and shoulders. Then her sweat started to trickle into her eyes, and she couldn't even drink in the view. Finally, she stripped off her t-shirt, stuffed it into her pack, and continued on, wearing only a sports bra and shorts.

Jake murmured appreciatively, and her warm skin heated to burning in response.

"We should rest," he suggested.

She stopped in her tracks, her hands in fists on her hips, and turned to him. "What happened to one foot after the other?" She demanded.

Her breath caught in her chest as his eyes slid over her body. Pure, naked desire dilated his pupils. She watched his Adam's apple bob as he swallowed hard, never looking away from her.

"We'll make better time if we rest awhile."

"Rest, huh?" She couldn't take her eyes off his parted lips.

"Something like that." A lazy grin spread slowly over his mouth and he reached for her hand to pull her off the trail and into a grassy field surrounded by fragrant blooming flowers.

They'd made love slowly, tenderly. Usually they had energetic, acrobatic sex. But not this time. This was gentle, like a whisper of wind kissing her neck. Reverent.

Three thousand miles and ten years away, Chelsea's skin was on fire. Despite the frigid wind whipping her hair. Despite the cold, gray day. She was molten.

"You need help," she told herself as she quickened her pace. If nothing else, her daydream had given her a burst of much-needed energy.

She didn't have to limit herself to fantasies about Jake. He'd made that abundantly clear. He still wanted her. And heavens knew, she still wanted him. It would be so easy to melt into his arms and spend the rest of her life making up for lost time.

But.

But she was a different person than that girl Jake had known. And he was different, too. More serious, less impulsive, and frighteningly sure of himself. Maybe they wouldn't mesh anymore. What if there was too much water under the bridge? What if too many years had passed? Did love have an expiration date?

These were good questions, good reasons to proceed with caution. To take it slowly and see what developed. But they weren't the real reason. The truth was that Jake West had shattered her when he left. She'd broken apart into a million little pieces, and the process of putting herself back together had—not to put too fine a point on it—sucked. It had sucked royally. She'd felt empty and closed off for a long time after Jake enlisted and left her alone on a Mexican beach. The fear of falling apart again, of undoing all the work she'd done, it was paralyzing.

She could almost hear Olivia telling her that being guided by fear was no way to live. And Liv was right, Chelsea knew she was. Look at her. She'd had the relationship from hell, trapped in a marriage with an emotionally abusive, cold, cheater. And she had been trapped for years. The CIA had told her she couldn't leave Mateo. That experience would make anyone skittish. But not Liv. She had jumped right in with Trent, never looking back.

Could she do the same? Did she have the nerve?

Her rumination was interrupted by the sweetest sound in the world—the distant growl of a car's engine. She turned her eyes skyward and issued a quick prayer to anyone who might be listening that the driver was a sweet old lady on her way to the grocery store and not a hunter hauling a bunch of his rifle-toting buddies to the game lands for some deer hunting and day drinking. Although, in truth, she was in no condition to be picky. She'd probably hop in a car with the Son of Sam if it meant she could lean her head back and rest for a few miles.

She turned back and stared at the road, willing the car to come into view. She made a futile effort to tidy her loose braids so she'd look less like a witch out of a folk tale and more like a hiker in need of a lift. She pasted a smile on her face and waited.

The engine grew louder. From the roar, it sounded like her savior would not be a grandma in a subcompact. More like a pickup truck, she thought. She just hoped the hunters weren't too drunk. She squinted into the distance. A Jeep came into view.

"No. It can't be."

It couldn't be, right? Surely she'd knocked Vance out.

She stared at the approaching Jeep. It was coming fast, too fast. The driver was speeding. The Jeep *was* the right color. This *was* the road Vance would take if he were headed back to his terrible shack of a house, hidden at the end of a long, steep, unpaved path behind the old lumber mill. Her throat threatened to close, and she wheeled around, searching wildly for a good place to conceal herself.

The Jeep revved its engine. She began to shake. She had to hide. Now. But there was no place to go. She let out a strangled scream of frustration, then eyed the metal guardrail that separated the curving road from a deep ravine.

The Jeep was almost close enough to make out the driver, but not quite. If she couldn't see them, then they couldn't see her. Right?

She squared her shoulders, ran straight at the guardrail, and vaulted over it. She was mid-leap when the sound of the Jeep's deafening engine filled her ears. He was driving right by her. She curled into a ball and hoped she'd land softly.

She didn't.

She hit the crest of the hill with a thud, and her forward momentum kept her going. She rolled, feet over head, over and over, down the embankment. She came to a stop in a heap at the edge of the Falls River. She lay there, just breathing, for a long time before she tested her arms and legs. Nothing seemed to be broken. She inhaled deeply and yelped at the hot stab of pain that exploded on her left side, just beneath her heart. She prodded the tender area and cried out again. Nothing broken except for her ribs, she amended. She wasn't overly surprised. She was pretty sure she'd hit every rocky protrusion, tree root, and boulder on her wild journey down the hill. She flopped back and panted through the pain like a cat giving birth.

Time for a pros and cons list.

Pros: She was alive—that was the big one. Vance hadn't stopped. So he hadn't seen her. She hadn't knocked herself out. She still had a chance to get her hands on the communicator before Vance put the pieces together.

Cons: She was lying in a ditch with an indeterminate number of broken ribs. She was still more than five miles from town and the police station. She was going to have to drag herself back up the embankment, possibly on her hands and knees.

She closed her eyes and listened to the burble of the river as it rushed by, still swollen from the storm. The sound was oddly soothing. The Falls River had always been one of her favorite local spots. It had been the selling point when she was looking for a location for her store. Because the river ran right behind the outfitters, she could go wading or kayaking before or after work. And there was the flat crushed gravel running and biking path that ran alongside it.

Her eyes popped open and she stared at the water to her left, calculating. *The trail is on the* **other** *side of the river,* she reminded herself.

But it's flat, she countered. *So much easier than scrambling up the steep embankment.*

The river was shallow from here to her shop. Even overflowing from the storm, the water level wouldn't come higher than her waist for the most part. And a good part of it would be thigh high.

But the river's wide. And cold. It's November.

Yeah, but the river's not frozen, so it can't be **that** *cold.*

She turned her head and eyed the rocky cliff that stood between her and the road. Icy water or sheer uphill climb? She sighed and gingerly pulled her knees up to her chest so she could unlace her boots. Then she struggled to standing, biting down on her lower lip to keep from howling in pain, and slid her feet out of her boots. It took what felt like ages to bend and remove her socks and, more than once, she was sure she would pass out. But she didn't.

She rolled up her pant legs, tied her boots

together by their laces and hung them over her right shoulder, then braced herself and plunged her left foot into the frigid water. She gasped at the breathtaking cold. The sharp inhalation sent a surge of hot pain to her broken ribs. She almost welcomed the sensation as a counterbalance to the stinging cold working its way up her leg.

"Just do it," she said aloud. Her teeth were already chattering.

She gritted her teeth and forced her right foot into the river. Icy water swirled around her legs as she disturbed the surface of the water. She ignored her urge to hurry and inched forward, one slow step at a time. The prospect of losing her footing was enough of a deterrent to keep her pace careful and deliberate. She pushed through the water like she was in slow-motion as the greedy river grabbed at her clothes, weighing her down, down, down.

On land or off, it's still one foot after the other, she told herself. *Just keep walking. Keep walking.*

8

Jake glared at Officer Halloran and Chief Joe Markham through the miasma of red-hot pain that spread out over his skull like a cap. At least his vision had returned to normal. More or less.

The police chief seemed unwilling or unable to maintain eye contact with Jake. It's possible that was a result of the low rumble of a growl that Jake couldn't quite seem to suppress.

The chief turned to Trent and spread his hands wide in a gesture of appeasement. "Look, we can take a report about Ms. Bishop's disappearance. I'm willing to do that even though she hasn't even been missing a full twenty-four hours yet."

Trent's jaw hinged open. "The last confirmed contact with Chelsea was the emergency dispatcher. She called in a break-in in progress, Chief. Respectfully, the logical conclusion is that she interrupted the intruder and he grabbed her ...." He paused and cast Jake a sidelong glance, then said softly, "...or worse."

Markham shook his head. "That's a helluva leap, and you know it."

Standing a foot behind and out of his chief's field of vision, the rookie Halloran pulled a face as the response. Jake silently agreed.

He broke in. "Is it, though? Her client took off with four million dollars. Thugs came all the way down from Boston to track him down and, presumably, kill him. You processed those guys. They're dangerous. And they certainly aren't working alone."

Markham opened his mouth to respond, but Jake steamrolled over him. "Vance Asher apparently checked himself out of the hospital AMA."

"AMA?" Halloran's pen hovered over his notepad.

"Against medical advice," Trent supplied.

Halloran's head bobbed, and he resumed his scribbling.

"When Officer Halloran here went to the outfitters to get Chelsea's statement about the break-in, she wasn't there."

"The sign said 'Closed for Lunch,' didn't it, Halloran?" The chief pivoted to the side and eyeballed his officer.

"Y-yes, uh, yes, sir."

He turned back to Jake and Trent. "She's allowed to eat, isn't she?"

Jake ignored the disingenuous question. "I already told you, Chelsea's cousin stopped by the store this morning. Chelsea wasn't there. Asher told her Chelsea asked him to cover for her."

"See? Ms. Bishop's last contact was just this morning with Vance."

Trent's jaw tightened. Jake knew the feeling. They weren't accustomed to being stonewalled by the local PD. If anything, the department usually bent over backward to assist Potomac. So, why the stiff-arm now? What was Joe Markham's problem?

Jake switched gears. "According to Vance."

"And we just told you, Chelsea's car is hidden

under a tarp on Asher's property. That's probable cause," Trent insisted.

Markham scoffed, "Probable cause for what?"

Jake stared at him for a long moment. The crowded office was silent save for the scratching of Halloran's pen across paper. Markham's eyes flitted away again, this time over Trent's shoulder and to the clock on the wall. He was getting ready to boot them out.

"For a warrant to search Asher's property," Jake replied in the most even tone he could muster.

"There's not a snowball's chance in Hades that a judge would sign a warrant on your say-so."

Ah, there it is. The heart of the problem. The chief's protecting his turf. He already has the feds breathing down his neck over the Royce Reynolds disappearance. He's not about to cede any ground to a private firm. Not even one that fills his department's coffers and helps out behind the scenes now and then with no recognition or renumeration.

Jake almost smiled. If it hadn't been for the vise grip on his head, he probably would've grinned. Now that he knew Joe Markham's unspoken need, it was the easiest thing in the world to appeal to it.

"Of course not," he agreed smoothly.

He felt Trent's curious gaze on him as he continued, "And I would never dream of asking you to secure a warrant on the word of two private citizens like Trent and me."

Ignoring the fact that this was exactly what they'd done, Trent caught on and jumped in. "That's why we came to you. To report what we saw. That's all. You know we don't meddle in local matters, Chief."

Halloran's head was nodding in agreement like he was a bobblehead figure.

The chief pursed his lips. "Sure seems like you're meddling," he said slowly. "Your attorney has been bird-dogging my investigators. And here you two are, skulking around Vance Asher's land, playing detective. What gives?"

"I think you know Ms. Bishop is a client. She hired us to find Mr. Reynolds and Mr. Asher."

"Which you did, at least partially. She didn't hire you to find *her*."

The mental leap was baffling. He didn't point out that she didn't need to find herself. *She* presumably knew where she was. *They* didn't.

"You know my fiancé, Olivia Santos, don't you?" Trent asked.

"Sure. The family has that big house out on the lake. Mom's some kind a political bigwig."

"And you know Chelsea's her cousin, right?"

"Yup."

"Olivia hired us to find her," Trent said in his most convincing voice.

It was mostly true.

Jake stared at the two police officers.

"Well ..." the chief waffled.

Jake jumped on the opportunity. "Just send Officer Halloran out to Asher's place with us. He can see it with his own eyes and draw his own conclusions. If he thinks the situation merits a warrant—or at least a knock on the door and a conversation with Vance, then great. If not, so be it."

He stretched his mouth into an approximation of a smile. Or he hoped he did, at least. It felt more like a grimace. His mind was fogging up again. Too much talking. Too much standing. He needed to get out of here before he collapsed.

"Hmph. Well, I guess that'll be all right. Halloran, go with West and Mann here.

Remember, you can only get a warrant on the basis of what you can see from Old Mill Road. No trespassing." He shot Jake a look.

Trent frowned. "Hang on, that path down to the house isn't Vance's property. I looked it up. It was owned and maintained by the lumber company, and they sold it back to the county when they ceased operations."

Jake touched his head gingerly. "You know, Trent, the county sure hasn't been maintaining it. That trip down the path scrambled my brain pretty good. Hope I don't have permanent injuries."

"You'll be darned lucky not to. You hit your head pretty hard." Trent managed to keep a straight face.

Chief Markham's mouth creased down in a deep, unhappy bow as he imagined explaining a lawsuit to the county board of commissioners. "Right. Halloran, *after* Mr. West signs a waiver of his right to sue the county for any injuries he's sustained, you take these two gentlemen over to Asher's and let them show you what they saw— from the path. You don't set foot on Asher's property or make contact with him without radioing in to me first. We clear?"

"Crystal, sir."

"Good."

"Thanks a lot, Joe." Jake pumped the chief's hand vigorously. "Let me know if you have any of those raffle tickets for the Officers' Benevolent Fund."

"I'll do that, Jake." Markham flashed a genuine smile, happy to have the natural order restored. He turned to Trent. "Hope we'll see you at the next Hot Rods and Hotcakes gathering."

Trent grinned back. "You know I wouldn't miss it."

The niceties out of the way, Jake cocked his head toward the door. "Come on, Halloran, look lively."

Jake and Trent exited the station with Halloran trotting along behind them. Trent muttered that they had a deal and that Jake was supposed to get himself checked out before they did anything else.

Jake pretended not to hear him as he stood outside Halloran's squad car and rattled off Vance's address. "It's hard to find, so follow Trent. I'll make sure he doesn't lose you."

He hopped into the passenger seat of Trent's ride and buckled his seat belt.

"I know you heard me."

He blew out a breath. "You heard Markham. He's not in the mood to cooperate, we have to take what we can get when we can get it. As soon as we get Halloran out there to corroborate that Chelsea's car is hidden under that tarp, we'll go straight to the clinic."

Trent gave him the hairy eyeball.

Jake sighed. "I mean it, Mann. You won't have to twist my arm."

Satisfied, Trent started the engine. Jake leaned back against the headrest and closed his eyes.

9

The swirling water lapped at Chelsea's waist, splashing up under and inside her insulated jacket. She wanted to keep as much of her clothing dry as possible, but she couldn't raise her arms over her head thanks to the searing pain from her busted ribs. So she waded across the river with her arms outstretched in front of her as if she were an extra in "Shaun of the Dead."

She laughed aloud at the absurd image. The sound, at once hoarse and high pitched, rose on the wind. Her laughter died on her lips as the wind kicked up the water and a wave hit her in the midriff. That's when she began to shake and tremble. The rapid, jerky movements seemed as if they'd never end, so she kept moving.

And when the uncontrollable shivering suddenly stopped twenty minutes later, she rejoiced. Her constant shaking and chattering teeth had made her progress much slower than it otherwise would have been.

"Maybe now I ... go a li'l *fashah*." She said the words aloud and frowned.

They sounded wrong. Was she slurring her speech? She couldn't tell.

The effort of holding her arms out became too much, and her shoulders drooped. Her hands flapped limply into the freezing water, and her boots slipped off her shoulder and landed in the river with a splash.

"Get ... the ... *booos*," she scolded herself.

No. Too tired. She lurched forward as her hiking boots sank under the water's surface and disappeared.

So tired. She should close her eyes and rest. *But only for a minute.*

She could let herself sink into the water, stretch out her arms and float across to the other bank on her back. *So relaxing. Just let go. Slide into the water.*

In some distant corner of her mind, an alarm bell was ringing. Faintly at first, then louder and louder, until the insistent high-pitched chirp hurt her ears and made her head ache.

Someone needs to change the batteries in the fire alarm.

She frowned and looked all around her. She was standing in the Falls River. There was no fire alarm.

Then what's that noise?

It's a warning, she answered herself. *Think. What's it mean when you stop shivering?*

You're not cold anymore.

Her inner voice scoffed. Her inner voice sounded an awful lot like her bossy cousin. *What's it mean when you're standing in the middle of a river on a windy wintry day?*

She screwed up her forehead and thought hard. Then she smiled triumphantly. "I know this one! It means you have hypothermia, and your body's shutting down."

Right, dummy. Your core temperature is below ninety degrees. Get out of the water! Get out of the water now!

She sighed, and her eyelids shuttered, her eyelashes fluttering down and kissing her face.

Yeah. Get out. In a minute. Gotta take this heavy jacket off, though. Slowing me down.

She fumbled with stiff, cold fingers with her zipper but her clumsy movements failed to move the zipper.

*You have hypothermia. You're going to **die**. You're going to die in this stupid river, Chelsea. Get out of the water!*

"*Shtop* yellin' at me, Liv!" she shouted, her voice dying on a gust of cold wind.

It was just like Olivia to yell at her. Like that time they stayed at the lake house for Liv's twelfth birthday. They'd been jumping off the hillside into the swimming hole, and Liv freaked out because Chelsea did a backward flip into the shallow part.

"*You're going to **die**. You're going to break your stupid neck in this stupid water and die. And then I won't have a best friend anymore!*"

Now, Chelsea laughed. Olivia was so dramatic. She didn't die. See?

She stretched her arms out to her sides and arched her back like she was king of the world.

"See?" She demanded to nobody.

She pushed out her chest, pulled her arms back further, and raised her face to the sky. And then, without warning, she pitched forward. She closed her eyes and leaned into the forward momentum, letting it pull her down. She told herself it wasn't the end of the world. She could do the dead man's float and rest for a while. She waited for the water to splash up over her face as she fell forward.

Instead, her face hit something hard. Really hard. Mud filled her nostrils and mouth, mixing with the blood she could already taste. Her chest, belly, and legs hit next. Rocky, dirty, land.

Land?

She turned her face to the side and opened her eyes. She'd face-planted on the river bank. She could see the trail from here. She struggled to remember why that was important. She wanted to do ... something. Follow the path to ... somewhere. She frowned as the information she was searching for danced in front of her, just out of reach. She could almost grasp it. And then it was gone.

She dug her fingers into the wet soil and pulled herself forward so that her lower body came out of the water. *Her side hurt for some reason.* Her bare toes caught purchase on the rocky bank. *Where were her shoes? Something was very wrong. She should get inside. Call Liv. Or Jake.*

She army-crawled forward another body length then paused to rest.

What made her think of Jake after all these years?

Jake's back. Remember? You shared a sleeping bag with him.

An image flashed behind her eyes. Jake's body pressed against hers, his hot skin a contrast to the damp, cold air.

Through the icy grip of hypothermia she could swear she felt Jake's body heat even now. *But Jake wasn't here. Besides, they hadn't been near the water; they'd been inside. She could see rough walls ... and stalagmites and stalactites. It was a cave?*

The cave. Right. We shared the sleeping bag when we went to rescue Vance in the wilderness.

Vance.

Her eyes widened as her fuzzy brain fed her bits and pieces of the last twenty-four hours. Oh, God. Vance. The basement. The flash drive. The holly bushes.

She had to get to the police station. *That's* why she crossed the river. She pushed with all her strength, her arms shaking from the effort, and raised her upper body. Shooting pain brought back another memory. Vance's Jeep speeding toward her. Then curling herself into a ball, diving over the guardrail, and tumbling down the embankment. Broken ribs.

She panted, open-mouthed, and continued to push up, ignoring the heated poker stabbing her in the ribs. She staggered to her feet and swayed. She was wobbly, like she'd had a few too many drinks. But she was standing.

She lurched to the crushed gravel path and frowned down at her bare, bloodied feet. Why wasn't she wearing shoes?

Focus.

Which way to town? She lifted her head and scanned the trail for a clue. There. The big, old elm tree with the V-shaped limbs that had made the perfect spot for a scrawny pre-teen Chelsea to climb up and settle in with a book for hours. The branches formed a seat, and if she leaned back against the tree's trunk she could see the railroad crossing outside of town.

She circled the tree and peered up. Her reading nook was on the left side of the tree. So town must be that way. She clung to the decades-old memory as she began to walk along the trail.

The sharp, small pebbles dug into her soles, stinging like thorns. She had a cloudy idea that the pain was a good thing. It meant she had feeling in her feet. After several paces, she stepped off the path and walked alongside it in the frozen grass instead. Every few feet, her brain would plead with her to stop. To rest. But some deeper, ancient part of her urged her forward.

Keep putting one foot in front of the other. Just keep walking.

10

J ake blinked. Closed his eyes. Opened them and blinked again. Nothing changed. He muttered under his breath, "Sonofa ...."

Beside him, Trent leaned forward and peered through his binoculars as if he could will the Forester back into existence. "I don't understand."

It seemed impossible. But there it was—or wasn't—right in front of their eyes. Chelsea's Forester was, contrary to their representation to the police chief, most definitely not tucked away under a tarp back behind Vance Asher's shed.

Oh, it *had* been. The tarp was still there, flung up against the side of the shed, flapping in the wind as if it were taunting them. If a tarp could say *na-na-na-na-boo-boo,* this one was.

"I don't understand," Trent insisted.

Jake cut his eyes over toward Officer Halloran, who stood a few feet away, right at the very edge of the access road. He had drawn as close as humanly possible to Asher's property line without crossing the boundary. He'd bounded out of his Crown Vic like a big Labrador retriever puppy, eager and anxious to chase down a tennis ball. Then he'd screeched to a halt, comically, when he'd reached the boundary line.

Now, the police officer looked neither eager nor comical. He looked profoundly embarrassed. Not for himself, but for them. He must've felt Jake watching him. He turned and scared up a sheepish smile.

"Obviously Asher came back and moved it," Jake said too loudly, ostensibly talking to Trent.

His eyes never left Halloran's face. To his credit, Halloran didn't look away.

"I guess," Trent agreed slowly. "Only ... wouldn't he have passed us on Old Mill Road?"

He was right, Jake realized. There was only one road that accessed the old mill site, and they'd just traveled it. If Vance had retrieved the Forester, he would've driven right by them after leaving his property. There's no way they'd have missed him.

"Not necessarily." Halloran's tone was confident—almost assertive, even.

Jake studied the rookie cop. Any police officer worth his badge would have dismissed Jake and Trent as crackpots after having been dragged out to this forlorn corner of the county to stare at ... nothing.

"What are you saying?" Trent asked.

"I'm saying if he was hiding Ms. Bishop's vehicle—and let's say for the sake of argument he was—he wouldn't want to be seen driving it around the area, right?"

"He makes a good point, Jake."

Halloran's cheeks pinkened with pride and he smiled.

"Where is he then?" Jake demanded. "He didn't vanish into thin air and take a thousand pounds of metal with him."

"Well, there's that ATV trail that goes through the woods behind the old mill and comes out in town. Matter of fact, it comes out down behind the outfitters."

Jake stared. "The Falls River Outfitters? Chelsea's place?"

"That's right."

"Do you know anything about this trail?" Jake asked Trent in a low voice.

"No. The only trail I know of behind Chelsea's shop is the hiking and biking path that runs parallel to the river. But, then again, I don't go four-wheeling."

Neither did Jake.

"Is this an active path? Is it passable this time of year?"

Halloran nodded vigorously. "Oh, yeah. I was just riding out there with my brothers and our buddies last weekend. It's muddy, but definitely drivable. I mean, don't get me wrong—it's bumpy, but no bumpier than the access road we just drove down."

"That's pretty bumpy," Jake said dryly.

Trent snorted, "You're never going to let it go, are you?"

"No. At least not before the goose egg on my head goes away."

"Fair." Trent turned toward Halloran. "And Asher would be able to get through in Chelsea's

Subaru? It's all-wheel drive, not four-wheel drive."

The officer knitted his eyebrows together and his eyes got a faraway look. After a long moment, he nodded. "He could do it. It wouldn't be a fun ride, but yeah, it's doable."

Jake punched his hand into his fist. "I think you're on to something, Halloran."

Trent slapped Halloran on the back enthusiastically, and the officer grinned.

As quickly as it had come, his smile faded. "But it doesn't make sense. Why move it at all? This is a great location to hide a car. I mean, look around. Nobody comes down here without a reason. And by moving it, he's risking running into somebody. After he went through all the trouble to stash the car, why not just leave it here?"

Chalk up another point for Officer Halloran. Jake looked at him more carefully. He wasn't quite the simple country boy he pretended to be.

"If he saw us or heard us when we were out here earlier, he could have panicked for some reason," Trent suggested.

There was a long silence. The wind whistled through the long grass. Nobody spoke.

Fine, he'd say it. "A reason like he's got Chelsea stashed in the house."

Halloran cleared his throat. "Before you even ask—"

"I know. You don't have probable cause for a warrant to search the premises," Jake said flatly.

Trent gave Jake a meaningful look. "We should stop wasting Officer Halloran's time and let him get back to the station."

"Right."

Halloran wasn't fooled. He knew exactly what they planned to do the moment he left. His internal struggle played out on his face as he weighed following procedure and following a lead. He shifted his weight and huffed out of breath. "I guess that's right. The chief's probably already wondering where I am."

He made the right decision. Prowling around Asher's property without a warrant was not only illegal, but career-limiting, too. Jake would never fault an officer for following the law. Now he just needed to get rid of Halloran so he and Trent could bend that law to the breaking point.

He stuck out his hand. "Thanks for your help, officer."

Halloran gave it a shake and cast a final

longing glance at Asher's place. Then he slumped his shoulders and started toward his patrol car. Halfway there, he stopped and turned.

"Hey, I've got some of Ms. Bishop's things in my trunk. You want to take them?"

"Things?" Jake frowned.

"Uh, yeah. The feds dusted everything for prints or swabbed them for DNA or whatever it is they do. The only thing they want to hang on to is that broken oar. I'm supposed to drive this stuff over to your offices and give it to Ryan Hayes. But you can sign the receipt, right? I mean, it's your company."

It was, indeed, Jake's company. And whatever else she was or wasn't, Chelsea was his client.

"Sure."

He followed Halloran around to the back of his black and white. Halloran popped the trunk and Jake glanced down at a box full of camping gear—backpacks, canteens, headlamps, and the emergency communicator that Vance had left in the woods. Halloran heaved the box out of the trunk and shoved it into Trent's arms, then handed Jake the sheet of paper that rested on the top of the pile of stuff.

"This is just a document that lists all the

items and states that I turned them over to you and you accepted custody of them on behalf of Ms. Bishop. You want to inspect it and make sure everything's there?"

Jake eyeballed the box and glanced back at the form. "Everything looks to be in order."

If it wasn't, Ryan would let him know.

Halloran slammed the trunk shut and handed him a pen. Jake held the paper against the car's trunk and scrawled his signature where indicated.

Halloran stuffed the form into his log book. "Thanks. When I get back, I'll scan this and email you a copy."

"Just send it to Ryan, if you would."

"You bet."

Trent popped the door and dumped the box on the back seat. As Halloran opened his driver's side door, Trent called to him, "Be careful getting out of here. Your brakes are probably soft. You're liable to slide on this loose gravel."

"Thanks. You know I have to tell you guys not to go poking around on Asher's private property."

"We know you do. And you just did," Jake assured him.

Halloran hesitated, clearly reluctant to leave.

Trent added, "You should get back. Look at it this way, the chief's gonna bust a gut when you tell him what a pair of dopes we are."

Halloran's lips twitched as he tried, and failed, to hide a laugh.

They all knew he'd be holding court at the bar for weeks with the story of Jake West and Trent Mann taking him out to a crime scene and ending up holding their metaphorical dicks in their hands. Potomac cast a large shadow over the valley, and local law enforcement lived in that shadow. Halloran wouldn't have to pay for a beer for the foreseeable future if he played up how wrong Jake and Trent had been. The fact that they all knew the Forester had been there was immaterial.

Halloran tapped two fingers to his forehead in an abbreviated salute and climbed into the car.

Jake and Trent watched the patrol car spin its wheels, then wheeze, and finally lumber up the hill with a high-pitched whine. Halloran paused at the entrance to the road, flashed his lights and blipped his siren. Jake raised a hand and waved as the car vanished from sight.

Jake and Trent turned back to the house and stood in absolute silence for a moment.

After a beat, Trent said, "Did you hear that?"

"You mean that faint crying, like maybe an animal's trapped in Asher's shed?"

"Animal? I was thinking it sounds more like a kid."

"Yeah, on second thought, you might be right. We'd better go knock on Asher's door."

"It'd be negligent not to," Trent agreed.

In unison, they stepped off the access road and into a legal gray area.

11

The sun peeked out from behind a heavy gray cloud, and Chelsea turned her face, closed her eyes, and basked for a moment. But only for a moment. She'd found that stopping was a dangerous game. As long as her numb feet were moving—however slow and painful her progress might be—she could focus on her goal. But when she rested, even just to catch her breath, the insidious, tempting thoughts began to swirl in her mind. The ideas were a whisper, but she heard them:

Stop and rest. Sleep. Just give in to the cold. Lay down. Relax. Someone will find you.

She opened her eyes and stumbled on. She'd

lost her bearings miles ago. In her delirium, the familiar landmarks all looked wrong, just a bit off. But she knew she had to be coming up on the town. The trees became more spaced out, and the faint hum of traffic grew louder. She was close, but how close?

The idea of overshooting her goal and coming out of the woods after she'd already passed the police station brought tears to her eyes. She was spent. She couldn't take extra steps. Better to leave the path now and walk through town. Even if Vance saw her, he couldn't do anything out in the open in the middle of the day. Could he?

She shrugged. She'd take her chances. She didn't have a choice.

She gathered the scraps of energy left in her dwindling, nearly empty reserves and sprinted up the hill toward the road. Or, she tried to sprint. The best her wobbly legs managed was a slow, shuffling jog. She pushed forward, panting and sweating.

She felt the change in her gait as the grass gave way to sidewalk. She'd made it. Tears trickled from her burning eyes and ran down her cheeks. She kept running. Off the sidewalk and into the street. She turned her head from side to side and spotted the gas station. She hadn't gone too far, she hadn't passed the police station.

Still crying, she stopped in the middle of the road to pump her fist in celebration. Her sobs turned to laughter, an uncontrollable laughter that shook her shoulders. She wiped the tears from her cheeks with the back of one hand and turned just in time to see a bright yellow sports car speeding toward her.

The driver's mouth was open in an 'O' of horror. Chelsea froze as if she were rooted to the spot and stared. She recognized that face. The car was almost on top of her when she squeezed her eyes shut and stiffened her body, bracing for the impact that was definitely coming. The car would slam into her any second. There wasn't time to stop.

I'm sorry, Jake. I tried.

The thought ran through her mind in the instant before the car plowed into her. She found it fitting that her last conscious thought would be of Jake West.

Only it wasn't. The car didn't hit her. Instead,

a cacophonous screech of brakes filled her ears and the acrid scent of burning rubber filled her nose. She opened her eyes. The front bumper of the car was inches away from her thighs. She could feel the heat from the engine on her legs.

Through the windshield, she locked eyes with the horrified driver.

Leilah, she thought. *It's Leilah.*

Then the world went dark, and Chelsea swayed—one, twice—then crumpled to the ground.

Jake waited until Trent was in position at the rear of the shack. Then he raised his fist and pounded on Vance Asher's front door.

Bang. Bang.

He listened hard. No movement came from the other side of the door.

Bang. Bang.

Nothing.

He crossed the rotting wooden porch and peered through the grimy window. No lights on inside. No television blared out from within the dark interior. He tried the door. The knob jiggled in his hand. Locked, but with a cheap, easily broken mechanism. He jumped from the porch to the rocky yard. The smooth motion concealed the jarring pain that thudded in his head when he made contact with the ground.

He ignored the flash of pain and rising nausea and jogged around to the back of the house. Trent stood on a rickety pile of lumber, looking through a window.

"Anything?"

Trent turned, then bent into a crouch and leapt down from the woodpile. "No. Nobody's home. How do you want to play this? The door's locked, but one halfhearted kick would take care of that." He jerked his head toward the door.

Jake considered their options. Trent was right. They could let themselves into Asher's house without breaking a sweat. The lock on the back door looked to be even flimsier that the one at the front of the house. They could take advantage of Vance Asher's sloppy home security. But if they busted in, they'd be giving Asher his pick of legal defenses to keep anything they found inside out of evidence. They'd also be breaking multiple laws themselves.

Ordinarily, Jake tried to stay on the right side of the law.

But Chelsea could be in there.

He stared at the door and listened to his heart hammering in his chest. He had this idea —probably stupid, definitely illogical—that he would *know* if she were in there. That some invisible connection tied them together, and he'd be able to feel her presence.

Definitely stupid, he informed himself.

Trent eyed him, waiting.

He cleared his throat. "Let's take a look at the shed first."

Maybe they'd get lucky. Maybe Vance left his shed unlocked. Maybe they'd find something there.

Trent shrugged and headed toward the shed. Jake trailed him, rolling his neck from side to side as if that would somehow dislodge the pain in his head. He gulped down the fresh air, breathing hard, as pain flashed behind his eyes.

Jake could hear Trent speaking but couldn't make out the words. The sound was distorted, almost like he was underwater. He turned to tell Trent to speak up, and saw that he was talking on his cell phone. Before he could ask who Trent was talking to, the world began to spin, then went dark.

I'm sorry, Chelsea. I tried to—

He hit the hard ground with a thump before he completed the thought.

12

J ake came to in a bright, white noisy space. He turned his head. White curtain, mechanical beeping, the sound of wheels rattling over the floor as equipment was wheeled from place to place, and loud, fast talking. The unmistakable antiseptic smell that permeated every triage center from a mobile medical unit in the desert to a level one trauma center in a U.S. city.

He was in an emergency room. He raised his right hand to his face and studied the plastic bracelet around his wrist, trying to make out the small print.

"We're at the university hospital."

He turned his head toward the voice. Ryan

Hayes sat in a molded plastic seat jammed in between an IV stand and a heart monitor.

"Where's Trent?" He croaked thickly.

His brain was foggy and heavy, and he had a headache that defied description. He felt hungover, but he knew he hadn't been drinking. He blinked hard, trying to remember what he *had* been doing. Something with Trent. That much he knew.

"I sent him back to the office. I told him I'd babysit you until you woke up. Figured it's better that I'm here anyway, in case the cops show up." Ryan studied him from behind his glasses.

"The cops? Why?"

"How much do you remember?"

"Bits and pieces. We were at Vance Asher's place and Trent took a phone call. I don't know why we were there, but that's the last thing I remember."

"You were looking for Chelsea. Or Asher. Either one. According to Trent, your working theory was that he grabbed her up. And that call Trent took was your buddy Officer Halloran calling to give you two a head's up."

"Halloran? About what?"

Ryan ran a hand through his hair. "Vance

Asher turned up at the police station, bleeding. Someone bashed his head in."

A memory flashed in Jake's mind. Asher in the cave, his head bloody. "Again?"

"Yeah, again. And according to Asher, it was Chelsea."

Jake lurched upright. "Chelsea? He admitted he has her? Where is she? Is she okay?"

Ryan rose and pushed Jake back into the bed. "Don't do that. You have a concussion. You have to stay in bed. He didn't admit anything. According to him, he was taking a lunchtime stroll through a holly bush thicket when she came out of nowhere and cracked him in the head with a rock."

"That's a load—"

"Yeah," Ryan said dryly. "Even Halloran realized it was pure fiction. But apparently, the chief was taking him seriously. So—"

"The police are looking for Chelsea?" That was good, actually.

"Probably. But they aren't going to find her."

Jake stared at him. "I'm missing something. How do you know they won't find her?"

"Because she's upstairs in the ICU. She came

in as a Jane Doe, and I figured we'd keep her name to ourselves for now."

"She's in the hospital? How do you know? Is she okay?" He raised himself to his elbows.

Ryan gave him an unamused looked and pressed him flat on his back with one palm. "Dammit, Jake. Stop trying to get up."

Jake struggled against Ryan's hand, but it was no use. Ryan was putting his full weight into holding him down. He could try to take him out. Ryan was a big guy, but he was a lawyer. Under ordinary circumstances, Jake could lay him out flat, no problem. But ordinarily, bright flashes of light didn't zing through his visual field and pulses of electric pain didn't course through his skull. He stopped moving.

"Okay, you win. I'll lay here if you tell me what the hell is going on."

Ryan nodded but kept his hand on Jake's chest, just in case.

"Leilah was driving back from a meeting in Northern Virginia. She stopped at Charlie's Gas and Go to refill her tank. When she pulled out, a sopping wet, barefoot woman staggered out into the road in front of her car. Thank God it was Leilah driving and not a civilian, because she stopped with inches to spare. She said most anyone else would've hit her."

Jake nodded. Leilah Khan was a professional race car driver. She could stop on a dime.

"And the woman?"

"The woman collapsed in the road. Leilah got out to check on her and realized it was Chelsea."

Jake jerked up. Ryan seemed to be expecting a reaction because he raised his hand from Jake's sternum and held up his palm like a crossing guard.

"She's going to be okay. She has hypothermia, some broken ribs, and a bunch of superficial injuries. She's in the ICU as a precaution because her core temperature got so low."

"And she hasn't said what happened?"

"Leilah called me from the car while she was bringing Chelsea here. She said Chelsea was drifting in and out of consciousness and was talking the whole time. By then, Trent had called to tell me *you* collapsed in Vance Asher's yard and he was bringing you here. He was worried about TBI."

Traumatic brain injury. That *would* explain why he felt like death on a plate.

"I think it's just a concussion."

"And since you're not a neurologist, we'll just wait for an expert's opinion. Anyway, he also told me what Halloran said. I used my keen legal mind to put two and two together and told Leilah to make sure Chelsea kept her mouth shut when she got here."

"You don't believe Asher's story, right?"

Ryan scoffed. "Of course not. But if Halloran's right, and the chief bought it, we need to find out what really happened before they learn that Chelsea's here. So, I gave Leilah clear instructions to keep Chelsea from talking to the medical team. Leilah's babysitting her to make sure she stays quiet."

Jake nodded gingerly. "Sounds like a good plan. Thanks for springing into action."

"Of course." Ryan's eyes were somber. "This is messy as hell, but once Chelsea's stabilized and can tell us exactly what happened, we can clear it all up."

"Right." Jake coughed weakly and gestured toward the plastic pitcher of water that sat next to a plastic cup on the table behind Ryan. "Could you ...?"

Ryan jumped to his feet and turned his back to grab the pitcher.

The moment he turned, Jake swung his legs around and launched himself out of the bed. He sprinted out the door, his hospital gown flapping open behind him. He knocked a tray of medical instruments to the floor with a clatter as he skittered around a corner. Behind him, Ryan was bellowing a string of obscenities.

Jake dodged an orderly and kept running.

13

Chelsea knew she should be paying attention to what Leilah Khan was telling her. She could tell by the serious look in Leilah's lively dark eyes and the slight frown creasing Leilah's mouth that it was important. But she was so tired and, finally, *finally,* warm.

The room was dimly lit and the blanket covering Chelsea's chest was heavy. She just wanted to sink back into sleep. Her eyelids dropped. Could she maybe listen with her eyes closed? Leilah grabbed her hand and kept talking in a fast, urgent voice.

"Mmmm," Chelsea answered.

She wanted to tell Leilah that she couldn't pay attention to whatever she was trying to tell her. The pain medicine the nurse had given her was making her sleepy. If Leilah would just stop talking, Chelsea could take a nap and then—

The door banged open. Someone shouted out in the hallway. Leilah shrieked and dropped her hand. The sound of fast, heavy breathing filled the room. She heard her name.

"Chelsea!"

The voice was thick with emotion. She knew that voice. She opened her eyes.

"Jake?"

Jake West stood in the doorway, panting. He wore a hospital gown and a stricken expression. He stared at her for a beat, then rushed across the room.

"Are you okay?" He breathed. He pushed her hair back out of her eyes.

She nodded.

"Jake, you're not supposed to be out of bed," Leilah protested.

He glared at her, then growled, "I'm fine, and I'm not going anywhere." He turned back to Chelsea and said in a tender voice, "I'm not leaving you."

She smiled up at him. "Thank you."

Leilah huffed and arched one eyebrow. Then she kicked a metal chair, and it slid across the floor toward Jake. "Fine, whatever. But could you at least sit down so I don't have to look at your naked butt hanging out of that gown."

Chelsea giggled. Jake made a sheepish face, tucked the gown around his thighs, and planted himself in the chair.

"Do you have a tattoo of ... green feet on your behind?" Chelsea leaned forward.

Jake either didn't hear her or pretended not to. He turned to Leilah. "Is she really going to be okay?"

"Yes. Everyone who comes in says she's doing great. To be honest, at this point I think they're keeping her mostly because they think she has amnesia. But Ryan said not to let her tell them who she is, so I don't—"

The door flew open again, and Ryan Hayes appeared, frowning and out of breath.

"Speak of the devil," Leilah said.

Ryan shot her a quizzical look.

"We were just talking about you," Jake explained. "About how you don't want Chelsea to give the hospital her name."

"It's a temporary solution. Until we can come up with a plan."

"A plan for what?" Chelsea asked.

"How much do you remember?" Ryan answered her question with one of his own.

She frowned. "Everything. I think?"

Jake leaned forward, eager and focused. "Start with the last night. After you left The Falls."

She thought hard. "Jake walked me to my car." She paused and remembered how he asked her to give him—no, to give *them*—another chance. Her face heated at the memory of the passion in his voice.

He coughed. "After that."

Leilah and Ryan exchanged a look. What was *that* about, she wondered.

"Okay, I was driving home along Falls Road. As I rounded the corner by my store, I spotted a light on inside. It caught my eye because it was wrong."

"Wrong?"

"I don't leave any lights on inside. It's a waste of electricity. And even if someone else locked up, the light was in my office. Nobody goes in there except me."

"Does anyone else have a key?" Ryan asked in a very lawyerly voice.

"Um ... only Vance."

The air in the room electrified when she spoke Vance's name. And a slew of memories rushed back. She started talking faster, wringing the scratchy cotton sheet between her hands as the words rushed out. "I pulled into the lot and called 9-1-1. I told them there was someone inside, a break-in in progress, and the dispatcher said someone could come out in the morning."

She fell silent.

"You went inside, right?" Jake prompted her.

She didn't answer.

Jake opened his mouth, but Leilah stopped him by putting a perfectly manicured hand on his wrist.

"Look at me," Leilah demanded.

Chelsea shifted her gaze to meet Leilah's eyes.

"I'm a business owner, too, right? If I saw someone inside my garage, messing with my cars, messing with *my business*, damn straight, I would've gone inside. Especially if the authorities blew me off. Whatever happened after you went inside, *it's **not** your fault*." Leilah's eyes seared into hers and her voice shook with conviction.

Chelsea swallowed hard and managed a tremulous smile. "I did. It's like Leilah said. I couldn't just walk away."

Ryan nodded. Jake clenched his jaw and cracked his knuckles.

Leilah prompted her. "What happened when you went inside?"

"I was all keyed up. I remember thinking I could grab a cross-country ski, use it as a weapon. Then ... I saw who it was. It was Vance. I was so relieved, and I felt so silly."

Anger at the memory of how embarrassed she'd felt swelled in her chest.

"Totally understandable," Leilah murmured. "He's your trusted second-in-command, yes?"

"Yes. Or he was."

"So, it'd be like Jake walking into the Potomac offices and seeing my brother, or Trent, or Ryan. He would think nothing of it."

"Yes," Chelsea said through tears. "Exactly."

She spared a glance around the room. Ryan was leaning against the wall, his long legs crossed at the ankles, his arms folded across his chest. He was watching Leilah with a bemused expression.

Jake was still sitting on the edge of his chair as if he were spring-loaded. He gripped his hands together so tightly that the veins in his forearms popped out. He stared at her intently. She wriggled uncomfortably under the ferocity of his gaze.

"Go on," Leilah urged in a gentle voice.

"He lunged at me, grabbed me by my throat. He was saying crazy things, talking about a flash drive. I didn't know what he was talking about but he didn't believe me. He kept squeezing my throat … and then I passed out." She drew a shaky breath.

Jake pounded his right fist into the palm of his left hand. A sound rose in his throat that she could only describe as a growl. Leilah frowned across the room at Ryan.

Ryan twitched his lips and crossed over to drop a palm on Jake's shoulder. "If you can't hear this, you can go out in the hall. But it's important for Chelsea to tell us as much as she can."

He squeezed Jake's shoulder. Jake nodded and cleared his throat, then gestured for Chelsea to go on.

"Anyway, I woke up in ... I mean, really, it was basically a cell. A room in his basement. He told me he was going to keep me there until I told him where this flash drive was."

"Did he say what was on the flash drive? Why he wanted it?"

She shook her head. "No. He said the men who have Royce threatened to kill him unless he gave it to them."

Jake and Ryan begin speaking at once, loudly, their words overlapping. She couldn't make out what either of them was saying, and then both increased their volume as if that might help. She tossed Leilah a helpless look.

Leilah stuck two fingers into her mouth and emitted a piercing whistle. Jake and Ryan both fell silent.

"Sometimes working with boys comes in handy," she said to Chelsea with a playful wink. "One at a time, please." She pointed to Ryan. "Lawyers first."

"He told you someone's holding Reynolds hostage?" Ryan asked.

She pursed her lips and clicked her tongue against her teeth as she tried to be as careful as possible in her response. "He told me that's what he thinks. Someone got to him in the hospital and threatened to kill him if he didn't get them this flash drive. He believes they have Royce Reynolds, and he doesn't have the drive on him, so ..."

"So it's either in the woods or you have it," Jake finished.

"Right."

A cloud of worry crossed Leilah's face. "They got to Vance in the hospital? *This* hospital, right?"

The four of them exchanged long, wordless looks. Chelsea's heart raced in her chest.

After a beat, Jake grabbed her hand. "Nobody's getting to you. Do you hear me?"

The heat and conviction in his voice eased the icy grip of fear that was threatening to strangle her. She smiled. "You're pretty sure of yourself for a man who isn't wearing pants."

Ryan coughed to cover up his laugh, but Leilah threw her head back and howled. Jake shook his head and gave her an indulgent smile.

"Anyway ..." he prompted.

"Anyway, I convinced Vance that the drive

must still be in the wilderness, so he took me out there and—"

"And you beat the devil out of him with a rock and ran for it," Ryan suggested.

She gaped at him. "How'd you know?"

Ryan cleared his throat. "He went to the cops. He says you jumped him without provocation. There's a BOLO out on you. That's why I told Leilah not to let you give the hospital your name."

Heat rose in her chest. "*I* attacked *him? They* want to arrest *me?*" Her voice shook with outrage.

"I know," Ryan said. "It's absurd. And we're working on a plan. Just tell us what happened after you got away from him."

She recounted as much as she could. The hike along the road, seeing Vance's Jeep bearing down on her, leaping over the barrier. Then the tumble down the hill, the icy river crossing, and finally collapsing in front of Leilah's bright yellow Porsche.

She gasped, "I'm so glad you found me." Tears welled in her eyes.

Leilah smiled and came around the bed to push Chelsea's hair out of her face. "So am I."

Chelsea took a deep breath and looked at Ryan. "What happens when the hospital finds out who I am?"

He didn't answer. "And you don't know anything about this flash drive?"

"No. Oh, wait. Yeah, I think it must be in the satellite communicator. There's a compartment that can hold an extra battery. If you take it out, there'd be room for a drive. And it's the only thing that makes sense." She turned to Jake. "Remember how the communicator was sitting out in the open on that rock? Like it was waiting for someone to find it?"

Jake shot out of his chair.

"Ass!" Ryan yelped, waving his hands.

Jake wrapped the gown around his butt.

"We have it. The communicator. Officer Halloran didn't want to drive all the way over to our offices to hand over a bunch of Chelsea's stuff that the feds didn't want. So I signed some custodial form, and he gave me the box. The communicator was in it. I saw it."

"Where is it now?" Chelsea asked.

Jake looked at Ryan.

"You gave it to Trent?" Ryan asked.

Jake nodded.

"Then it's back at Potomac."

Nobody spoke for a long moment. Finally, Leilah broke the silence. "So, now what?"

Ryan studied Chelsea's face for a long moment. Then he said, "That's up to Chelsea."

14

"Yes," Chelsea repeated for the third time.

"No," Jake bellowed, also for the third time.

Ryan kept his eyes on Chelsea and ran through the plan again.

Jake fumed. Why was nobody listening to him? He was a former pararescue specialist. A Medal of Honor recipient. He had not one, but two, Air Force Crosses. He was the owner and CEO of a multimillion-dollar corporation. Okay, he was also wearing a hospital gown and no skivvies, but did his pedigree count for nothing?

Leilah patted his arm as if he were a small child. He glared at her. She smiled sweetly and inclined her head toward the corner of the hospital room. He held his gown together in the back and shuffled after her.

"What?" He growled.

"Why are you here?"

He stared at her. "What kind of question is that? I'm in charge, last I checked. I'm the president and—"

"No. Why are you *here*? You know, with the band around your wrist and the no pants?"

He waved a hand as if he were waving away a fly. "I banged my head on the dash of Trent's SUV, and he was worried I have a TBI because I have a ... mild headache."

She pursed her lips and lowered her chin to look at him over the bridge of her nose. "Mmm-hmm. Right. And as the only person other than Trent who's likely to have actually bashed her head in a collision, I'm calling BS on your mild headache."

He opened his mouth, but she kept talking.

"I've already called Omar. He and Marielle are doing whatever nerdy things they do."

"Don't they just have to open the spare battery compartment?"

She shrugged. "Maybe. Omar started

babbling about extracting the drive from the emergency communicator and, well, you know ..."

"Your eyes glazed over?"

"Exactly. Anyway, Trent's working the Officer Halloran angle. Olivia's handling your meeting with that VIP. Ryan is explaining to Chelsea exactly what she needs to say and not say for this to work legally. No offense, Jake, but your job— your *only* job—is to stay out of everyone's way."

His mouth was still hanging open, but he found himself at a loss for words. He blinked at her.

Leilah laughed, not unkindly. "I know, you're a man of action. A take charge, alpha individual. And you're wounded. I mean, an utter idiot could tell from the way you look at Chelsea that you're completely besotted. But, you, my friend, are woefully misguided."

He blinked. "You don't ... she doesn't feel that way about me?" He wanted the floor to open up and swallow him as soon as he spoke the words, but he also, deeply, desperately, needed to hear the answer to the question.

She sighed, then took pity on him. "Oh, Jake. No. She very much feels that way. When she was regaining consciousness, your name was on her lips—"

He pumped his fist. She shook her head.

"No. Listen. She's not twenty anymore. She's a grown-ass woman. She rushed into a dangerous situation to protect her business. She kept her wits about her and got away from her abductor. She waded across a river with busted ribs and pushed through freaking hypothermia. Do you understand what I'm saying, Jake? If you treat her like a china doll, all you're going to do is push her away."

He dropped his hand and hung his shoulders, deflated. "But she's a civilian."

"So am I. So is Ryan. That doesn't mean we're useless."

He eyed her. "So, if it were Ryan, and not Chelsea, you'd be fine with it?"

She jutted her chin forward and her eyes took on a defiant glint. "Truthfully? I would. I remember when Trent sent Ryan into the colonel's house to steal his files. I was his getaway driver, remember? Was I worried? Yeah, of course. But, Jake, people rise to the occasion—unless you push them down and prevent them from doing it. And if you do that, well, they'll just grow to resent you."

She stared unblinkingly at him for a long moment.

Finally, he sighed. "Who knew you were such a philosophical race car driver?"

"I contain multitudes, Jake. Most people do. I'm telling you, let her do this. She *needs* to do this. And *you* need to learn how to let other people spread their wings."

She locked eyes with him until finally, reluctantly, he looked away first.

"Fine," he said, forcing the words out around the lump in his throat and not quite believing that he was agreeing to this, "she can be the bait."

15

Chelsea licked her dry lips and wrapped her fingers around Marielle's wrist like a crow clutching a branch. The data analyst-cryptologist-whatever-she-was smiled warmly and gently pried Chelsea's fingers away.

"Now, then, this itty bitty microphone goes into your bra—boop!—and nobody will see it, yes?" She snaked the thin wire down through the collar of Chelsea's shirt and tucked it into her cleavage. "And you don't have to activate it or say anything special. It will record all by itself. Genius, no?"

"Yes." Chelsea tried to strike a casual tone but failed miserably. It came out more like a pant.

Marielle smiled again and tried another tack. "You and I, we were Olivia's bridesmaids, yes?"

"Yes."

"And we knew Mateo, he did not deserve her?" Marielle spat on the floor.

Somehow, the vulgar gesture was both dainty and Parisian. How did she manage that, Chelsea wondered.

Then she laughed. "Yeah."

"And also we knew that we could not stop Olivia. She had to walk through the fire and come out stronger on the other side, no?"

Chelsea shrugged. It was true. Anyone who loved Liv could see that her relationship with the Mexican millionaire was a train wreck—if the train crashed into a dumpster fire. But, equally, they knew she would never listen to reason.

"*D'accord,*" Marielle said. "This is the same. You must walk through the fire or you will never put this experience in your past."

Leilah, who Chelsea could have sworn was busy telling Ryan what to do, jerked her head up. She met Chelsea's eyes with a fierce, fiery look. "Elle's right. You have to face off against this bastard Vance or he will haunt you forever."

Chelsea gulped and nodded. She had an

uneasy feeling that Leilah was speaking from personal experience.

"You're right. You're both right. I'm good. I'm ready." She bounced lightly on the balls of her feet like a boxer.

"You go, girl," Marielle said, eliciting a giggle from Leilah. "Now, take pity on Jake and talk to him before he explodes."

Chelsea took a stutter step toward the cluster of Potomac operatives. Either Leilah or Marielle gave her a much-needed push. She desperately wished Olivia were in the circle of operatives, but she forced herself to walk forward anyway.

The group was huddled around a map of the town, pointing and muttering. She plucked at Jake's sleeve and he drifted away from the others.

"You okay?" He asked, knitting his eyebrows together. "If you're having second thoughts, you don't have to do this."

"No, Jake. I do." She took a deep breath, then gestured toward his head. "Are you okay?"

"Yea, the neurologists gave me a clean bill of health. No brain bleeding or swelling found on the CT scan or the MRI. Trent was just being overprotective. I just rang my bell." He knocked on his head as if to demonstrate its sturdiness.

She scared up a smile. "I'm glad Trent insisted you get checked out. Brain injury's no joke."

He nodded. "And neither is what you're about to do." His expression was suddenly solemn.

"I know."

"You can still back out."

"Stop saying that. I need to face him. Besides, I know you won't let anything happen to me."

She said it lightly, but he grabbed her hand and searched her face intently. "Do you? Because I won't."

"I know."

"Chelsea ... after this is all over ..." he trailed off, biting down on his lower lip.

She leaned forward. "After this is all over, you and I should go on a date."

"A date?"

She wet her lips. "Yeah. A date. A real one."

He grinned. "You've got it, Bishop."

On the other side of the room, a walkie talkie crackled. Trent called, "We're a go. Somebody give her the drive!"

Ryan materialized from the crowd and

pressed a small, smooth flash drive into her palm. "You ready?"

She nodded. "Ready." Then she stepped out of the deli's back room, smiled at the confused Korean couple who'd reluctantly allowed them to take over the space, and walked out of the store and onto the sidewalk.

Omar's voice sounded in her ear. "You got this, Chels. Just be casual."

Casual, right.

She walked stiffly to the curb and waited for the light to change, keeping her eyes pinned on the police station on the other side of the street. *Trent arranged everything with Officer Halloran. Everything's going to be okay.* **You're** *going to be okay.*

She took a deep breath. And suddenly, she knew. She was going to be okay. The light changed, and she crossed the street. As she swiveled her head from left to right, she spotted him coming toward her.

"We see him. You're good," Omar assured her, his voice crackling in her ear.

She lowered her head and kept walking. When she was nearly in front of the police station, Vance stepped out in front of her. She couldn't believe he was being so bold. But, then again, as far as he knew, she was going to the station to turn herself in. Halloran had assured Jake that Vance bought the cover story.

"Vance," she said, not having to feign the surprise in her voice.

"Chelsea," he answered evenly. "Just give it to me, save us both the trouble."

"Give what to you?" She turned the drive around in her closed palm. It was already slick with sweat.

"Don't be cute," he snarled. "I know you're going to turn the drive over to the cops and turn yourself in. The chief called me in so I could identify you. Just give it up, already."

She sighed and shifted her gaze to her closed right hand, then hurriedly raised her eyes to meet his. "I don't know what you're talking about."

He laughed.

"You got him, reel him in," Omar whispered in her ear.

She visualized landing a struggling fish and leaned back on her left foot. Vance followed the movement. Then his gaze fell on her closed right hand and he grinned toothily, almost feral.

"I'll take that," he said, bringing his hand down in a chopping motion on her right wrist.

She opened her hand and let the drive fall to the sidewalk with a clatter as Officer Halloran burst out of the doorway to the printing shop behind Vance and tackled him as he reached for the flash drive.

Trent raced across the street and scooped her up, yanking her out of the danger zone while Halloran rolled Vance over and handcuffed him.

"What ... about the drive?" she panted as Trent pulled her to safety.

"It's a dummy," he said near her ear.

"A dummy?" Of course it was.

"Anyway, the thing in the communicator? It's not even a flash drive."

She twisted her neck to look up at him. "It's not? What is it then?"

"You'll have to ask Marielle or someone on her team. She told Omar it's a hard wallet, whatever that is."

"Hard wallet?"

"Something   something   cryptocurrency,"

Trent told her. "Come on, I'll have your cousin and Jake on my ass if I don't get you inside."

She followed him back inside the Korean deli in a daze.

16

C helsea was falling asleep into her bowl of bibimbap. Someone refilled her glass of wine, and she raised her head to say a sleepy thank you.

Olivia elbowed Jake in the ribs, sharply.

"Ow!"

She jerked her head. "My cousin's tired. Someone needs to get her home. She can't drive after the day she's had."

Trent leaned across the crowded table. "Well, neither can Jake. Dr. Chudharta said—"

"Dr. Chudharta said I'm cleared for all activities of daily living," Jake announced, loudly as he stood and pushed his chair back. "Mr. Min, Mrs. Min, thank you for the amazing dinner."

Their hosts nodded and smiled. He reached his hand out to Chelsea. "Can I take you home?"

She gave him a secret half-smile. He decided to take that as a yes. He slid his corporate credit card toward Ryan, who was giving some sort of lecture on hard wallets, and soft wallets, and crypto keys. Jake understood that this wasn't over. Whoever had Reynolds had the key, but not the safe that held four million dollars—or something like that. He might not grasp the nuances, but he understood that Chelsea was still in danger. Right now, though, she was tired. And he had priorities.

He tried again to shove his card at Ryan, who was still yammering.

"I got it," Ryan mouthed before launching back into his monologue about digital currency protocols.

Jake shrugged and tucked the card away. He offered his arm to Chelsea like he was some kind of eighteenth-century dandy. "Shall we?"

Chelsea waved goodbye to the group. Olivia raised an eyebrow, and Marielle blew her a kiss. But, Leilah launched herself out of her seat and enveloped Chelsea in a tight hug. Jake looked around while the two women whispered intently.

A moment later, Chelsea tucked her arm under his elbow.

"Ready?"

"Ready."

They stepped out of the deli and paused on the sidewalk. In unison, they lifted their faces to the dark night sky.

"New moon," she murmured.

"Mmm-hmm."

He kept his gaze on the stars. Even in town, there was little light pollution. Orion's belt blazed out of the dark. Venus twinkled above.

Chelsea snuggled into his side. "Remember the night we saw the Milky Way?"

As if he could ever forget. "Oregon, right?"

"Yeah."

They'd sprawled out on the soft carpet of pine needles and ogled the smeary purple and gold pinwheel of stars spreading across the black sky. Ten years later and three thousand miles away, they stared up at another night sky. Jake's heart pounded like it might leap right out of his chest.

"Yeah," he finally said, thickly.

After a breath, she whispered, "Jake?"

He turned his eyes away from the constellation-splashed sky and looked into her clear green eyes. "Yeah?"

"I ... really don't want to be alone tonight. Do you think—?" She trailed off and chewed on her lower lip.

He stared at her, his heart thumping. Was she kidding?

"Yes. God, yes."

Her face split into a smile that threatened to crack his chest in two and she slipped her warm right hand into his left. "Good."

His right hand reached into his pocket and patted the little velvet pouch that cradled the silver ring. Not tonight. But soon. Very soon.

~

Thanks for reading *Imperiled!* Ready for more Jake and Chelsea? Order Entwined, the next book in the series here!

THANK YOU!

Thanks for reading *Isolated!* Jake and Chelsea's story continues in Imperiled, available in late 2021.

Keep reading. Check out the first book in one (or all) of my four bestselling mystery and thriller series for free, available where books are sold.

Review it. Consider posting a short review to help other readers decide whether they might enjoy it.

Connect with me. Stop by my Facebook page, https://www.facebook.com/authormelissafmiller, for book updates, cover reveals, pithy quotes about coffee, and general time-wasting.

ALSO BY MELISSA F. MILLER

I've written *loads* of books! In addition to the
Shenandoah Shadows Series, I have four other series:

The Sasha McCandless Legal Thriller Series

The Aroostine Higgins Novels

The Bodhi King Novels

The We Sisters Three Romantic Comedic Mysteries

ABOUT THE AUTHOR

USA Today bestselling author Melissa F. Miller was born in Pittsburgh, Pennsylvania. Although life and love led her to Philadelphia, Baltimore, Washington, D.C., and, ultimately, South Central Pennsylvania, she secretly still considers Pittsburgh home.

In college, she majored in English literature with concentrations in creative writing poetry and medieval literature and was stunned, upon graduation, to learn that there's not exactly a job market for such a degree. After working as an editor for several years, she returned to school to earn a law degree. She was that annoying girl who loved class and always raised her hand. She practiced law for fifteen years, including a stint as a clerk for a federal judge, nearly a decade as an attorney at major international law firms, and several years running a two-person law firm with her lawyer husband.

Now, powered by coffee, she writes legal thrillers and homeschools her three children. When she's not writing, and sometimes when she is, Melissa travels around the country in an RV with her husband, her kids, and her dog and cat.

Connect with me:
www.melissafmiller.com

Made in the USA
Las Vegas, NV
16 July 2022

51669062R00094